MAIL ORDER MIRIAM

WIDOWS, BRIDES, AND SECRET BABIES

JENNA BRANDT

COPYRIGHT

Ms. Brandt writes from the heart and you can feel it in every page turned.

— SANDRA SEWELL WHITE,
LONGTIME READER

For more information about Jenna Brandt visit her on any of her websites.

Signup for Jenna Brandt's Newsletter

Visit her on Social Media:

www.JennaBrandt.com
www.facebook.com/JennaBrandtAuthor
Jenna Brandt's Reader Group
hwww.twitter.com/JennaDBrandt
http://www.instagram.com/Jennnathewriter

MAIL ORDER MIRIAM

A runaway Russian princess, a copper mine owner, and a secret baby that could ruin their chance at a happy marriage.

Miriam Novikoff leads a sheltered life as a princess until her husband is killed and she is blamed for his death. In order to keep from losing her head, she flees to America, with only a handful of jewels to pay her way to freedom. On her trip out West, she realizes she's pregnant, a complication she never planned on.

Mark Bennett owns half of the largest copper mine in all of Arizona. He enjoys running the family mine and spending time with friends when he isn't working. However, that isn't enough for his match-ing-making aunt, who insists he needs to settle down and find a wife. He doesn't want any of the women she's been throwing at him lately, so he decides to take matters into his own hands and places a mail order bride advert.

Can Miriam find a way to trust Mark with her big secret? What will Mark do when he finds out Miriam is pregnant? And what happens when Miriam's past catches up with her?

-To Connie-
Readers like you make it worth writing.

Early Spring 1884
St. Petersburg, Russia

*P*rincess Miriam Novikoff tried to focus on the feeling of freedom she felt when she rode her stallion, Ilari, at full gallop. She knew it was unladylike to ride astride with full abandonment as she did that morning, but she needed a way to release the frustration she felt over her husband's latest indiscretion.

She held her arms wide from her body, her chest thrust out over the horn of the saddle in a determined manner. Tightly, she gripped the reins, urging her four-legged friend to carry her as far away from the palace as possible. The more anger that crept into her heart, the harder she pushed her horse, not caring that it made it impossible for her riding companions and imperial guards to keep up with her. The palace staff insisted that she take a legion of servants with her wherever she went, but it didn't mean she had to like it.

"Your Imperial Highness, please, slow down," she heard one of the men call out from behind her. "You aren't safe riding like this."

Miriam was tempted to ignore the man's plea, but she knew the edge of the bluffs was fast approaching. Even though she wished for a way out of her miserable marriage, she refused to find it by giving up on her life. Her death would suit her husband's purposes too well, and she refused to give him the satisfaction.

With practiced ease, she slowed Ilari down from a gallop, to a canter, and finally, a slow trot. Her head lady-in-waiting, Karine, arrived by her side first, her face pinched tight from exhaustion. "Are you ready to return to the palace, your Imperial Highness?"

Miriam pulled out a handkerchief from her skirt pocket and wiped the sweat from her brow, dreading the thought of heading back to the gilded cage where she would have to resume playing her role of the Grand Princess of the Imperial Russian court. When her uncle, her only living relative, arranged her marriage to Grand Prince Nicholas, Emperor Alexander III's firstborn son and heir, Miriam thought a whole new world would open up for her. She imagined spending a life with a loving husband while enjoying beautiful balls and state dinners. Little did she know, what actually awaited her was being subjected to the maniacal whims of a spoiled, egotistical brute. For a year, she'd been forced to live with a husband who cared so little for her, that he regularly spent his nights out drinking, gambling, and carousing with other women. In hindsight, she knew it had been naïve to expect him to be faithful to her, but at the minimum, she wished he could at least be discreet. On a daily basis, she dealt with members of the imperial court, as well as the staff, giving her looks of pity. It was never discussed, but everyone knew how poorly he treated her.

"Let's stay out here a bit more, Karine. The fresh air does us both good."

"As you wish, your Imperial Highness," Karine deferred, refraining from pointing out that they needed to return within the next hour. Miriam was required to return in time to get ready for her mandatory duties.

Miriam dismounted from her horse, handing the reins to one of the guards. She meandered along the edge of the recently thawed creek, wondering what it would be like to stick her toes in the cold water. She didn't dare lift up her riding skirt and kick off her boots to do it. Oh, wouldn't it be nice to not have to worry about how her decisions reflected on her position.

"Your Imperial Highness, it's time we return to the palace," Ivan, her head guard stated firmly in a deep voice. "We have been out longer than intended."

Miriam glanced over at the burly dark-haired man. He had a worried look on his face. She suspected he was concerned about getting into trouble for not returning her promptly. Even though she didn't want to go back, it wasn't in her to cause someone else to get into trouble because she wanted to avoid her husband.

"I suppose you are right, Ivan. We wouldn't want to keep his Imperial Highness waiting." She took the reins of the horse and placed her foot in the stirrup, then pulled herself up and into the saddle. She ignored the footman that offered her the steps most noblewomen used to mount their steeds.

After returning their horses to the stables, Miriam made her way inside the ostentatious St. Petersburg residence of the imperial family. Between the dramatic use of columns and gold, there wasn't an inch of the place that didn't scream opulence. With hundreds of rooms varying from massive dining rooms to great halls, the palace could easily accommodate thousands of guests at a time. Tonight was no exception. The imperial family was hosting a masquerade ball for her husband's thirtieth birthday, and every one of note was invited.

Her ladies-in-waiting hurried her to her suite of rooms where they energetically worked to make sure her golden gown, made from the finest lace, was cinched perfectly at her waist. The layers of the skirt cascaded down and around her feet, as if it was part of a masterful waterfall designed just for her.

"Your gown looks spectacular," Karine gushed, adding several pieces of the imperial family jewels to accent her outfit. "You don't need these gems, but I know his Imperial Highness will want you to wear them."

Karine was too afraid to say it out loud, but they both knew the Grand Prince only wanted Miriam to wear the jewels so he could show them off. Her husband didn't think of her as anything more than a reflection of himself.

The ladies placed Miriam's dark hair into an elaborate updo, weaving pearls into the curls to match the ones around her neck. As a final touch, they added some rouge to her cheeks and lips, causing her alabaster skin to stand out strongly against her facial features.

As Miriam stared at herself in the mirror, she noted she looked every bit the princess she was expected to be. She just wished she could find a way to reconcile the person she hid beneath the surface with the woman she pretended to be for everyone else.

"Are you ready to go downstairs and take your place in the receiving line, your Imperial Highness?" Maria, her newest lady-in-waiting, asked with an eager smile on her face.

"I suppose it's that time, isn't it?" Miriam put on a brave face and headed towards the door. Before she reached it though, the door flew open from the other side.

Her husband's furious brown eyes glared at her as he marched into the room. "Out, all of you," he shouted at the other women, gesturing towards the exit behind him. "I need a moment alone with the Imperial Highness."

Miriam sucked in a deep breath and held it, her stomach clenching with dread as her ladies-in-waiting scurried from the room. Her husband rarely visited her chambers, usually only when he was drunk and in the mood to try to make an heir, or when he was upset with something she did. Neither reason ever bode well for her.

"Is something the matter, your Imperial Highness?" she asked as she moved over to her vanity and picked up her gold-dusted lace mask. She was hoping if she just let him yell at her without resisting, he would move on faster. She kept her gaze averted as she secured the mask over her eyes and across her cheeks, tying it firmly at the back of her head.

"Yes, there is. I thought we agreed you would visit me in my chambers last night," he barked out as he scraped his hand through his black hair. "I waited all evening for you."

"I'm sorry that I displeased you, but I didn't feel well last night." It wasn't a lie. Miriam had been so distraught over his last dalliance that she'd spent a restless night tossing and turning, to the point that she even felt physically ill.

"It doesn't matter; when I give you an order, I expect you to follow it," he growled in anger. "Not only am I your husband, but I'm the Grand Prince of Russia. I could have your head for not doing what I tell you."

The threat didn't surprise her. It wasn't the first time he made it, and part of her wondered if one day, he would carry it out. The Novikoffs were known for dealing harshly with anyone that chose to defy them.

"If you want, you can make it up to me now," he commanded, his hand snaking out and grabbing her roughly by the arm. "You'll have to be very, very convincing that you're sorry, though."

As he pulled her close, she could smell the alcohol on his breath. Apparently, he'd already started drinking for the evening, which meant he could prove to be even more noxious to deal with than she first thought.

Yanking her arm away from him, she snapped,

"I'm already dressed for the evening, and we have guests waiting for us downstairs."

"They can wait a little while longer," he snarled, reaching out for her, but she shrank away, stumbling backwards in the process. As she continued to move away from him, he kept pace with her, until her back smacked against the wall. She slid against the wallpaper until she reached the door that led to the balcony. She twisted the handle, and slipped through, hoping that the cool air might sober him up.

"You should know by now, there's nowhere to go," he warned. "I own you."

He pounced on her so quickly, she barely had time to blink before it happened. A yelp escaped her lips; the pain from where his hands were digging into her arms caused tears to fill her eyes.

Frantically, her gaze darted around, looking for anything that might help her escape. From the corner of her eye, she saw a flower pot. She squirmed free, not caring that his nails tore at her tender flesh as she pried herself loose. Without thinking, she picked up the ceramic pottery and slammed it against his head. His eyes widened in stunned shock for a brief moment before he crumpled to the ground.

Gathering up her skirts, she hurried from the balcony, hoping she could hide at the party until he found someone else to take his anger out on. She only made it down three corridors before she panicked and turned back around, fearing what would happen once he woke, or worse, if someone found him before he did. No one struck the Grand Prince and got away with it, not even his wife. No matter what happened, he would be furious. At least if she returned and begged his forgiveness, her punishment would be less.

Miriam entered her chambers and made her way back through the room, preparing herself for the verbal lashing she was sure to receive. As she approached the balcony, she stopped just shy of the door when she overheard the familiar voice of not only her husband, but his brother. They were arguing heatedly, causing her to pause. If she made her presence known, it would only make the situation worse. Instead, she peeked through the crack and listened.

"If you can't even control your wife, how are you going to rule this country, Nicholas? You're the Grand Prince of Russia, for heaven's sake, yet, you got pummeled by a girl a third of your size."

"I'll deal with my wife," her husband bellowed,

the rage clear in his voice. "And once I do, she'll *never* challenge me again."

Miriam shivered, knowing that he planned to punish her in the most severe of ways. She suspected he might even have her whipped privately for her transgression.

"Wait until the nobles hear about this; you'll be the laughingstock of the entire court," Constantine cautioned.

"You won't dare tell them," Nicholas ordered, the fear clear in his voice. "As your sovereign, I command you to shut your mouth."

"You aren't my sovereign yet," his brother pointed out, "and you never will be if I have anything to say about it. You are a disgrace to the Novikoff name; between your philandering and your drunkenness, you are going to end up destroying this family. I won't give you the chance, just like I'm not going to give you the chance to have our family deposed. You're not fit to rule this country."

"How dare you speak to me in such a way. I have a good mind to have you exiled for it," her husband threatened in his consistent style.

"You don't have the backbone; you never have."

"I told you not to speak to me that way."

Nicholas lifted his hand to strike his brother, but Constantine grabbed his hand mid-air. There was a struggle between the two men, and to Miriam's utter disbelief, Nicholas went tumbling over the side of the balcony.

Miriam screamed, traumatized by what she just saw. Constantine's attention shifted from the railing to her, his eyes narrowing into slits of hate.

Immediately, fear seized her heart, prompting her to slam the door shut and lock it before fleeing her chambers. She just witnessed the murder of the Grand Prince by his own brother. If she didn't escape now, she'd be the next to follow her husband over the balcony.

Miriam ran through the corridors of the palace, making her way down the staircase at the front of the residence, hoping she could blend in with the other guests dressed for the masquerade. She weaved through the crowd, keeping her gaze averted to avoid recognition until she could make her getaway.

Just as she reached the back doors that led to the veranda, she heard Constantine shout from the top of the stairs, "Someone find the Grand Princess; she's pushed the Grand Prince from her balcony."

Complete chaos erupted around her; everyone scurrying about as women screamed and cried and men cursed under their breath. Miriam took advantage of the pandemonium and slipped through the doors, rushing through the maze of garden paths. Lucky for her, she knew the paths well after spending countless evenings in them praying for her husband to stop having a wandering eye.

At the edge of the gardens, she found the gate unlatched. Before she could slip through though, she heard Ivan's familiar voice behind her. "Stop right there, your Imperial Highness."

Miriam spun around, the fear she felt in her heart unmistakably written across her face. "It isn't what you think, Ivan. I didn't do it."

"I'm not sure what you're talking about, your Imperial Highness, but you know I can't let you go anywhere without an escort."

To her surprise, Ivan wasn't with any of the other guards, but rather Karine, who was adjusting the bodice of her dress and pushing her hair back into place. It was strictly forbidden for ladies-in-waiting to have affairs with members of the guard. Why hadn't Miriam ever noticed before that Ivan and Karine were involved? Clearly, she had been so self-absorbed with her own tragic events, she didn't even notice what was happening right beneath her nose.

"If you let me go, I won't say anything about what is going on between the two of you," Miriam promised, gesturing towards them. "I just need you to let me pass without alarming the rest of the guards."

Karine and Ivan looked at one another, then slowly nodded their heads.

"Take care of yourself, and don't mention you saw me tonight. It will be better for the both of you." Miriam slipped from the garden and rushed along the back streets of the city, knowing that she had to forever leave behind her life as the Grand Princess of Russia.

2

Late Spring 1884
Little Ridge, Arizona

"You ready to head over to Uncle Martin's house for dinner?" Garrett Casner, Mark Bennett's brother-in-law, best friend, and mine foreman, inquired as he came into his office.

Mark stood up and stretched his arms over his head, tired from a long day at work. It was a mighty task to run the largest copper mine in all of Arizona, but at least he got to do it with his best friend. "Yes, I'm ready to go."

"Uncle Martin is going to be happy to hear that the mine production is fifteen percent higher than it was last month."

"Hiring those new workers was a smart call," Mark praised, grateful that when he saw his uncle for family dinner, he would be able to give his business partner a positive report. "You're a good foreman, Garrett, and I don't know what I would do without you."

"Well, now that Jonathan Bosley is out of the picture, you'll never have to worry about that again."

Mark knew that Garrett was trying to make light of what happened last year. The other man nearly got Garrett killed when he staged a robbery of the mine deposit. It had all but destroyed Garrett's relationship with Mark's sister, Becca. Garrett had temporarily lost his memories, spent time recovering from amnesia, and didn't return home until months later. Luckily, they were able to repair the damage and married as they planned, but it had been a long and arduous road.

"I'm just glad you're home where you belong." Mark patted Garrett on the back before locking up the office, then heading over to their waiting horses.

They rode the short distance into town and

made their way to the giant brick mansion that belonged to Martin Bennett. They entered the lavish home, filled with expensive mahogany furniture and precious antiques, and entered the dining room where the rest of the family was waiting.

"Glad to see you could make it. We've held dinner for the past hour," their Uncle Martin stated from his spot at the head of the table. He had a sour look on his aging face, as he pressed his thin lips together in frustration.

"Sorry about that, Uncle, but I had to finish up a pressing project at the mine," Mark explained as he took his seat next to his sister, Becca, and Garrett took the other empty seat beside her.

"The good news is you'll be happy to hear that the mine has had a fifteen percent increase in production," Garrett added with a wide grin. "And that's after paying the new workers."

The frown disappeared from the older man's face as he nodded in approval. "That *is* good news, indeed. We should celebrate." He waved for one of the servants to come over and ordered a round of champagne be poured for the entire table.

"I know that you men think the world revolves around money, but I'll have you know, there are some things far more important," their Aunt Claire,

Uncle Martin's sister, said from the other end of the table. The pair of older siblings were both widowed, and happy to remain unattached. They seemed, however, overly invested in making sure the younger Bennett family members were married off as quickly as possible. "Since I've already successfully matched Julia and Ed," she gestured across the table at Uncle Martin's daughter and her rancher husband, "And Becca and Garrett are happily married now, it's time for me to focus on my last remaining stubborn case." She turned her attention to Mark. "What do you say, nephew? I have a new prospect for you."

Mark let out a heavy sigh and crossed his arms over his chest as he unwillingly listened to his aunt go on and on about June Wentworth's sister-in-law. He thought when he rejected his aunt's last match, it would put an end to her meddling ways. It seemed like no matter how hard he protested, she couldn't seem to understand that he was content with his life as it was.

"She's excellent with children, since she regularly watches her nephew, Ben, as well as the new baby, while June works in the apothecary."

"She's pretty from what I hear, too," Uncle

Martin chimed in. "Which always makes a match easier to swallow."

"Aunt Claire, Uncle Martin, I'm quite capable of finding my own wife, if and when I ever choose to get married," Mark pointed out. "Currently, I'm far too busy with the mine to take on a wife."

"Oh, hogwash, Mark, there's always a reason to not get married if you look for one—you just have to jump in with both feet and take the plunge. I think if you just let me pick out a suitable match, you'll see—"

Mark stood from the table and threw his napkin down on the table. "That's it, Aunt Claire, I've had enough. I don't want to hear another word about a 'suitable' match for me. When are you going to understand, I don't want someone else picking out a wife for me?"

Without waiting to see how his words affected his family, he turned around and stormed off towards the exit.

He heard the rapid pattering of someone else's feet behind him, and before he could slip through the door, a hand reached out and pulled him around.

His own blue eyes met his sister's matching ones. "Don't run off like that, Mark. Aunt Claire didn't mean any harm by trying to set you up with a match. When Garrett disappeared, she tried to do the same thing for me."

"And as I recall, you absolutely hated every moment of it."

"I did, but I didn't take it out on Aunt Claire. Why don't you come back into the dining room and have supper with everyone?"

Mark shook his head, causing his sandy blond hair to swoosh back and forth. "I'd rather eat alone than have to listen to another minute of that. She swears every time she is done trying to match me, but she can't help herself. First it was the mayor's cousin, who is entirely too young, then it was Mr. Dulton's daughter, who has four children, not to mention a chip on her shoulder. After that, it was the pastor's niece, then it was some woman from Yuma. I'm pretty sure I'm missing a couple, but none of them were what I want in a wife."

"What do you want, Mark? You keep rejecting every woman Aunt Claire suggests, but you never give her anything to go on."

Mark pressed his lips together as he contemplated his sister's query. The truth was, he didn't even know what he was looking for, so how could he possibly explain it to someone else? It was easier to stay single than to settle for a match that would never make him happy. "I told you, I don't mind being a confirmed bachelor. The mine, not to mention our family and friends, keep me plenty busy."

"I don't think it's enough, Mark. You're missing out on love, and the chance of starting your own family. I want nieces and nephews to spoil one day."

"Julia will give you plenty of babies to fawn all over," Mark deflected. "Don't put that responsibility on me."

Becca shook her head. "You're just as stubborn as father was. He never admitted when he was wrong, either."

Mark leaned forward and kissed the top of his sister's head. "Give my best to everyone. I'll see all of you at church on Sunday."

As he made his way home to his own house, he thought about what just happened. His aunt was never going to stop; she just kept pulling names out of thin air like a magician. If he wanted this to end, he needed to take matters into his own hands. Didn't one of the miners mention placing a mail order bride advert in a newspaper?

When Mark reached his home, he marched

straight into his study and pulled out a piece of paper.

Several scribbled out attempts later, he finally had something that resembled what he wanted in a wife.

RESPECTABLE GENTLEMAN OF 28, with a good income from a copper mine, seeking marriage to a refined and virtuous young lady, who doesn't take herself too seriously. Must be accustomed to running her own home and staff as well as independent enough to keep herself busy. Needs to be able to engage in intellectual conversation as well as laugh at dreadful jokes. Should enjoy attending the theater and balls, but also content with a picnic by a river.

HE DOUBTED there was a woman out there that could fit his list of contradictions, but if she did, he hoped she found her way to read his advert. Either way, he would rather take matters into his own hands, than have to settle for a woman his aunt thrusted on him.

3

As Miriam stared out the window of the train at the passing sun-kissed canyons and plateaus, she pondered her own fate. Finding protection from the noble families loyal to her own had proven impossible; none of them wanted to be caught harboring the woman accused of murdering the Grand Prince. Her only choice was to sell the last of her jewels to buy two simple dresses and travel across the Pacific Ocean, praying for a way to start over where no one knew who she was. She had no idea, however, how hard that was going to be when she arrived in San Francisco. She was down to her last bit of money when another woman at the boarding house suggested looking into the *Matrimonial Times*. At first, Miriam had balked at the thought of promising herself to someone she'd never met, but as she became more desperate, the idea seemed less absurd.

For the hundredth time, Miriam wondered if she was making the right decision to accept Mark Bennett's offer of marriage. Despite being taught English by her tutor when she was young, finding reputable work for a woman was nearly impossible in America. Without being able to explain her education and noble upbringing, she couldn't use any of her references to obtain a governess or teaching position. Marriage to a stranger was the only thing that could keep her from either compromising herself or starving to death.

Miriam read through dozens of mail order bride adverts, finding fault with each one, before finally settling on the copper mine owner from Arizona. His advert seemed sincere, and he was of an age that was comfortably close enough to her own. He also had the means to take care of her— not that she had any expectations of anything resembling her old life. To have a home of her own with a kind man was more than she could hope for, given what she was running from.

Her stomach grumbled, reminding her that she hadn't eaten anything since earlier that morning.

Every time she thought about food, nausea overtook her and she found herself feeling faint. Perhaps she'd picked up a sickness along her travels, or she was still suffering from nerves after what happened to her in Russia. She just needed to get through this last part of the journey, and it would pass once she settled into her new home.

In the meantime, she needed to use the privy. She stood from her seat, knowing it was a long walk to the small room that held the commode. As soon as she did, however, everything around her started to spin. She reached out and placed her hand on the back of the seat to keep herself from falling over. She closed her eyes, trying to force the space around her to right itself, but it didn't help. Instead, bright flashes of light popped behind her eyelids, making the dizziness even worse.

"Are you all right, dear? You look rather pale?" Gertrude Pindle, who made it her mission to know all the other passengers on the train, asked from across the aisle. "Is there anything I can do to help you?"

"I'm sure I will be fine," Miriam mumbled in a Russian accent, but a fresh wave of nausea filled the pit of her belly, causing her to gasp as her eyes cracked open. She placed her hand over her mouth, worried that the little contents in her stomach might come spilling out at any moment.

"Are you sure? You look like you might be ill this very second. Do you have a fever?" the other woman asked as she stood up and stretched out her hand to feel Miriam's forehead. "Not one bit. What could be causing this?" The woman's eyes flickered down to her belly, then back up to Miriam's face. "Is there any possibility that you might be with child? You told me the other day that you were recently widowed."

Miriam's eyes widened incredulously as her hand fell from her mouth to her stomach. Was it possible that she was pregnant? She'd felt sick for weeks now, and she'd gone two months without menstruating. She'd assumed all of that was due to the stress from watching the murder of her husband and the loss of her home. Now she wondered if there was a completely different reason.

"I…I never thought of that until you brought it up," Miriam stammered in dismay, still trying to process the possibility. Tears formed in the corners of her eyes, prompting her to blink rapidly to keep them from falling. "I never imagined being pregnant under these circumstances. What am I going to do?"

"I didn't mean to upset you, dear; I know it's a lot to think about. I'm sure your fiancé will understand though." The elderly woman patted her on the arm, sympathetically. "Why don't you sit down before you faint; you're shaking."

Like a wooden puppet, Miriam did as Gertrude suggested. The woman sat next to her, rubbing her gently on the back.

Miriam swallowed several times, trying to force the lump to pass from her throat. How could she have let herself get into this situation? She'd only been intimate with Nicholas a handful of times over the past several months, but apparently, that was all it took. Even after his death, he'd managed to create endless problems for her. A baby complicated everything. The more she thought about it, the more obvious it became why she'd so firmly made herself believe she had been ill rather than accept the fact she was pregnant. By carrying Nicholas' child, the stakes for surviving were even higher. She'd barely evaded capture the entire time she was on the run. Once the imperial family knew she was carrying the heir to the Russian empire, however, they would stop at nothing to track her down. Once they found her, she would lose her baby to them. They took whatever they wanted by any means necessary. The only thing worse than that would be if Constantine found her first. He would order her execution to keep the Grand Imperial Crown for himself.

No matter how she looked at it, she was in a terrible position. Her only option was to throw herself at the mercy of her future husband, and pray he was the honorable and upright man she hoped he was. It wasn't like she could keep the truth from him. It was only a matter of time before her secret became obvious. Was he the sort of person that could raise another man's baby as his own, or would he reject her once he knew?

"Can I pray with you, dear?" Gertrude offered. "There isn't anything that the Lord can't help you with."

Miriam nodded, knowing that the other woman was right. She let Gertrude take her hands in hers as they both closed their eyes. As she listened to Gertrude whisper prayers of strength and encouragement, she tried to lean into her faith. She wanted to trust that God would somehow make a way for her and her baby to be okay.

4

After a thorough inspection of the plans for the latest expansion of the copper mine, Mark Bennett assured himself that everything was in place to break ground the following Monday. It had been a long day at the end of a very long week, but at least his plan was ready to be implemented.

Preparing for a major expansion had proven most difficult. Between assuring his miners they could continue to work during the expansion and maintaining production while organizing the new site, Mark was exhausted from weeks of twelve-hour days.

"Are you finished for the day?" Garrett inquired from the doorframe of the office.

"Yes, I was just finishing up." Mark placed the

papers back in their folder, then slipped them into his desk drawer. "I just need to check one more thing." Mark stood from his desk, wanting to go out to check the site of the new tunnel one last time for before leaving for the day.

"I told you, I've got it under control. There's nothing to worry about."

Mark knew better. Next week was going to test his endurance further than anything ever had. When the new team arrived ready to carve out a second tunnel into the mountain, his twelve-hour work days were going to switch into eighteen-hour ones.

"This has to go perfectly; Uncle Martin is counting on me."

Garrett nodded. "And it will, I promise."

"If one explosion goes wrong, it could take down the entire mine, not to mention the mountain."

"That won't happen. We have the best tunnel team in the country coming here. They know exactly what they are doing," Garrett assured him. "Are you ready to head out for the day?"

Mark nodded as he stood from his chair and picked up his suit jacket to put it back on. After adjusting his tie, he walked over to the coat rack and grabbed his hat, placing it on his head.

"Why don't you come over for dinner tonight? I'm sure Becca would love to catch up. You've been so busy lately."

"Thank you for the offer, but I need to head over to Yuma." Despite Garret giving him a probing look, Mark didn't give any further information. He wasn't about to reveal the fact that today was the day Mark's secret mail order bride arrived in Arizona. He needed to be at the Yuma train depot to pick her up in an hour, so time was of the essence. The last thing he wanted was to be late and start out on the wrong foot with his new wife.

Mark retrieved his carriage from home and ordered his driver to make haste. On the way to pick up his bride, he thought back to the letter he received from her. With no photograph and limited details about her life, he should have been skeptical of her correspondence. Something about her letter, however, resonated with him. He found himself returning to it over and over again. Within two days after receiving it, he was sending her back a telegraph with an offer of marriage.

He pulled it from his coat pocket and read

through it again, determined to convince himself that he was doing the right thing.

Upon reading your advert, I wished to propose myself as a possible partner for your endeavors. Not only can I fulfill your requirements, but provide even more than you ask. With a petite frame of 5 foot, fair complexion, and dark hair and eyes, I think you will find my appearance pleasing. I'm musically inclined, playing both the piano and the harp for over a decade. Additionally, I'm a skilled dancer and equestrienne, devoted to my faith in Christ, and fond of helping others whenever possible.

Widowed after only a year of marriage to a rather rotten man, I find myself wanting to find a husband worthy of giving the rest of my life to. I wish to be with a sober man, incapable of a wandering eye, as my last husband broke my heart with every breath he took. When I realized there was no future for me in Russia, I came to America, hoping to establish a new life for myself. I hope to one day have children to dote on, and plan to be an excellent mother, given the opportunity.

P.S. Here is a dreadful joke for you: Why is a dog like a tree? Because they both lose their bark once they're dead.

. . .

YOURS TRULY,

MIRIAM DOBROW

WITH A NOD OF HIS HEAD, the letter did its trick and reassured him he was making the right choice. A dark, foreign beauty with a playful sense of humor was exactly what he needed, harkening back to his memories of the Russian governess who had been like a second mother to him.

The carriage pulled to a stop at the train depot and his driver opened the door for him. "We've arrived, Mr. Bennett. I'll be waiting. Just send the porter along with the baggage."

"Will do, Hucksley," Mark said as he climbed down. He made his way over to the wooden platform just as the train pulled up. He let out a sigh of relief, grateful that he got there before his bride.

Anxiously, he watched as people exited from the cars. About five minutes into the unloading of the passengers, an attractive brunette in a blue daydress floated down the metal steps. He couldn't take his eyes off of her, and he immediately found himself drawn towards the gorgeous woman. The closer he got, the more intoxicating her allure became, making him giddy with the thought she might be his soon-to-be wife.

"Excuse me, ma'am, but do you happen to be Miriam Dobrow?"

The woman's head swiveled to the side, her gorgeous chocolate eyes settling on him. As he stared into them, he noticed that they had a touch of auburn in them that matched the sun-kissed streaks in her hair.

"I am Miriam Dobrow," the women stated with a small smile. "Are you Mr. Mark Bennett?"

"Yes, Mrs. Dobrow, I am indeed your intended husband." He gave a slight bow of his head. "Pleased to meet you, and since we're getting married, I think you can call me Mark."

She gave a nod in return. "Then you should address me as Miriam."

He could tell she wasn't sure what to do next as she shifted her tapestry bag from one hand to the other.

"Here, let me take that for you," he offered, reaching out. "I'll have the porter grab your other luggage and have it delivered to my waiting carriage."

"That won't be necessary. This is all I brought with me."

Mark glanced down at the small bag that now rested in his hand. This was all she had? He knew she left Russia to come to America under less than ideal circumstances, but he had no idea she'd left with so little. Even a widow would have had some sentimental trinkets and clothing she would have wanted to bring along, wouldn't she? What could have happened to her to spur such a departure?

Even though tons of questions rolled around in his head, he knew it wasn't the time or place to ask them. He wanted his future wife to feel like she could trust him, and questioning her like a criminal would have the exact opposite result.

"Well, then there's no need to wait any longer," he stretched out his free arm, offering it to her. "Why don't we head back to Little Ridge so we can get married."

"Right now?" she sputtered out, her eyes widening with disbelief. "I was hoping we'd have some time to get to know one another first. Perhaps I could stay at a hotel for a few days."

"I'm sorry to say, there isn't much accommodations for guests as small as the town is, so to make sure it's proper for you to stay with me, we have to be wed straight away."

Miriam's eyes fell to the ground as her body stiffened beside him. He could tell she was uncomfortable with his plans, but he knew it was the only way it was going to work. If his aunt found out that he was planning to marry a stranger, she'd find a way to stop it. This would only work if he married Miriam before any of his family knew.

"I understand your apprehension, but my home is plenty big enough for the both of us to live there without getting in each other's way. I have several guest rooms for you to pick from, and four servants that live full-time in the home. You have nothing to worry about."

His explanation seemed to ease the tension. She relaxed and let her eyes drift back up to meet his. "Thank you, I appreciate the lack of pressure you're putting on me. I have to admit I'm not used to it."

Her odd statement made him wonder what her life had been like back in Russia. Had her husband been an oppressive tyrant that ruled over her? Was that why she seemed so skittish with Mark? Was she not used to being around a kind and considerate man?

They reached the carriage and he helped her inside, then climbed in next to her. "I don't know what your previous life was like, Miriam, but you'll always be safe with me; I give you my word."

On the ride back to Little Ridge, she didn't speak. He wasn't sure if it was because she was shy, or if she was hiding something. Either way, he had a hard time breaking the ice with the woman. Whenever he asked her a question, she gave the shortest possible answer, and never followed up with a question of her own. By the time they arrived in town, he knew as little about her as he did before. It should worry him, but somehow, he found it more intriguing than terrifying to be marrying a woman he hardly knew. He was always up for an adventure, and he had a feeling marrying Miriam Dobrow was going to prove to be the grandest feat of his entire life.

Miriam watched her fiancé from the corner of her eye as they made their way from the livery down Main Street. She hadn't expected him to be nearly as handsome as he was. She'd just hoped that he wouldn't be so ugly she found him repulsive, but when he approached her at the train station, she'd nearly lost her breath when she saw him. With his wavy blond hair, bright blue eyes, and sculpted face, he was strikingly handsome. His good looks were only enhanced by his tall, chiseled frame, causing her own petite frame to be magnified. It had been all she could do not to let her mouth fall open as she stared at him.

"Is there anything you need before the ceremony? Would you like to change into a different dress?" Mark asked from beside her.

She shook her head. "I only have one other, and this is the nicer of the two by far." She hoped he didn't press her for further information, and was relieved when he didn't question her lack of belongings.

"Well, blue's quite a lovely color on you. It reminds me of the deepest part of the river."

"Thank you." She smiled at him, pleased that he didn't mention the fact that it was a simple dress made of cotton, and entirely plain for such an occasion as a wedding. She didn't have much of a choice, considering her other gown was faded from age, and had a hole at the elbow. Paying to have it fixed was out of the question, which left her to do the work. She'd planned on mending it herself once she had the know-how and supplies, but between her morning sickness and exhaustion from travels, she never was able to manage the chore.

As they moved down Main Street, she noticed people turned to stare with curious expressions on their faces. She wondered if it was because she was new to the town, or the fact that she was walking with her hand resting on Mark Bennett's arm. It was a small town after all, with only a few stores and homes sprinkled along the dirt streets. She suspected it meant the residents knew everything happening around the place, and paid attention when something out of the ordinary was going on.

Mark opened the front door to the white wooden church, and gestured for her to enter. "Let's get inside before someone works up the nerve to stop us and ask what's going on."

It confirmed that Mark was just as aware of the prying eyes as she was. She hurried into the small building and glanced around, not sure what to make of the place. Her family, as well as the imperial household, attended services at Saint Isaac's Cathedral, a building as opulent as it was grand. With bronze doors, marble and granite statues, and scores of paintings by Russian master artists, the cathedral was a far-cry from the minimalistic church that held no more than a dozen wooden pews, a simple altar at the front, and a handful of stained-glass windows to let in light.

Mark guided her down the aisle, where an average looking man with a kind smile waited for them. "Welcome, both of you," he greeted as they came to stand in front of him.

"Thank you, Pastor Murphy. May I introduce my intended wife, Mrs. Miriam Dobrow."

"Pleased to meet you." The man gave her a nod, then turned his attention to Mark. "You mentioned that you wanted to get the ceremony underway as soon as you arrived, Mr. Bennett, but are you sure you don't want your family here for such an important moment in your life?"

Mark waved off the other man. "No, this is a private matter, and I want to keep it that way. My family will just try to talk me out of it, and I've made up my mind."

"It's your choice, but I had to ask," Pastor Murphy said with a frown. "I hope your uncle doesn't run me out of town for going through with this."

"I won't let him," Mark vowed. "He's more bark than bite, anyhow."

Miriam wondered what she'd gotten herself into. It sounded like her future husband's family wasn't going to be happy about their nuptials. Was she making the right choice by going through with this? She had enough problems of her own that she didn't need to be adding to her list a hostile extended family.

Her hand fell to her belly, and she reminded herself, she didn't have just herself to consider. She was terrified what would happen if anyone back in

Russia found out about her condition. It was paramount that she made this situation work in order to provide a safe home for her unborn baby.

If this marriage was to happen though, shouldn't she enter her marriage with no secrets between herself and her husband? She wanted to trust Mark and tell him of her condition, but all of the men she'd ever known had proven disloyal. Her uncle had sold her off to the imperial family to increase his own influence, and her husband had done nothing but repeatedly betray her. If she told her almost-husband about the baby, would he be different from the rest of the men she knew, and follow through with his pledge to her? She was scared to take the chance, but she knew she owed him the truth before he committed to her. She would hate for him to think she tricked him into marrying her, knowing that she was pregnant with another man's child.

It was a rather big risk, as he could reject her on the spot, but Miriam was determined to do the right thing. She sucked in her breath and held it, pushing back her shoulders as she opened her mouth to tell Mark her secret. Before she could utter the words, however, a pretty young blonde woman with an angry scowl threw open the doors and marched inside.

Miriam's eyes widened with shock as her mouth went dry. What on earth was going on? Who was this woman and why did she look like she was fit to be tied? Was she a jilted lover coming in to claim her right to Mark? And if so, did that mean Miriam was going to soon find herself without a groom?

6

"Mark Bennett, you better have a good excuse why you're in here with that woman, in what looks like a wedding ceremony. I could barely believe my eyes when I saw you from across the street. I can't believe you actually went through with it and ordered up a bride," the blonde woman accused, moving towards him as she wagged a finger at him. "I thought you were joking about that when you mentioned it, but here you are, proving me a fool to think you had any common sense. You have no business promising your life to a complete stranger."

"What's the difference between this and what Aunt Claire wants me to do? The results would be the same; me married to a woman I don't know. At least this way, I get to do the picking," Mark countered.

Becca flipped her hair over her shoulder in annoyance. "Aunt Claire didn't mean any harm by her matchmaking, and you know it. This is just your way of retaliating out of spite, but think about it, Mark, this isn't something you can take back once you do it. It's forever."

"I know that," he said, crossing his arms over his chest defensively as his eyes narrowed into slits. "And I don't need my know-it-all sister sticking her nose where it doesn't belong."

"Don't you dare act like I don't have the right to be involved in your life. You sure didn't have a problem telling me I shouldn't take Garrett back after he returned home last year."

"And I admit, I was wrong about that, just like you're wrong about this." Pulling Miriam towards him, he added, "If you can't accept what I'm doing, you should leave. I don't need you here." A hurt look crossed his sister's face, and he realized he'd crossed the line. She spun around and started to take off the way she came, but he hurried after her. Mark jumped in front of his sister, blocking her path. "I'm sorry, Becca, I didn't mean that. After

Mother and Father died, you were the whole world to me. Please don't go."

She looked up into his eyes skeptically. "You're sure? You want me to stay?"

He nodded, reaching out to touch her arm. "Of course I want my only sister at my wedding, but you have to respect my decision. Do you think you can do that?"

She pressed her lips together and she slowly nodded her head. "I just want you to be happy, Mark."

"I appreciate that, and I promise you, this is for the best. You'll see."

They both made their way back over to where Pastor Murphy and Miriam were watching them.

"Miriam, may I introduce you to my sister, Becca Casner."

"It's a pleasure to meet you," Miriam said with a small smile. "I never had a sister; but am looking forward to that changing."

"So am I; welcome to the family," Becca gushed as she reached out and pulled the other woman towards her, who had a shocked look on her face as Becca did it.

Once Becca released Miriam, she moved over and took a seat in the front pew. Mark took Miriam's hands in his own, then leaned forward and whispered for only his bride to hear, "Sorry about all of that. My sister can be a lot to handle, but she has the biggest heart of any person I know."

Pastor Murphy started the ceremony. "We are gathered here today in sight of God to unite in the bonds of holy matrimony, Mark Bennett and Miriam Dobrow. Do you, Mark Bennett, take this woman to be your lawfully wedded wife? From this day forward, to have and to hold, for better or for worse, for richer and for poorer, in sickness and in health, until death does part you?"

"I do," Mark promised.

"And do you, Miriam Dobrow, take this man to be your lawfully wedded husband? From this day forward, to have and to hold, for better or for worse, for richer and for poorer, in sickness and in health, until death does part you?"

"I do," she committed in return.

"Now, it's time for the exchanging of the rings. Please take the rings you've selected and place them on each other's fingers and repeat after me: 'With this ring, I thee wed.'"

Both the bride and groom did as they were directed, slipping on the gold bands and repeating the promises.

"In so much as the two of you have consented together in holy wedlock before God, I now pronounce you husband and wife. You may kiss your bride."

Mark leaned towards Miriam, pausing for a moment before deciding to kiss her on the cheek. He didn't want to make his new wife uncomfortable by choosing the more intimate act of kissing her on the lips. He hoped in time that might come to pass, and was a patient enough man to give her the time she needed while he waited.

"Thank you for letting me be a part of this," Becca said as she came up to them. "I can't say it was how I expected to spend my afternoon, but you've always been one to keep me on my toes, Mark." Turning to Miriam, she added, "You both have to come over for supper tomorrow night. I won't spoil your big announcement and tell the family, but you should probably head out the back door of the church if you don't want someone else to do it."

Taking Becca's advice, the newly wedded couple snuck out the back of the church and made the short walk over to Mark's house on the edge of town.

When they entered his home, his robust, salt-

and-pepper-haired head maid, Mary, rushed up and fussed over them, taking Miriam's shawl and Mark's top coat. "I had Tandy put all of your belongings away in the rose room, Mrs. Bennett. It's by far the prettiest of the guest rooms and it overlooks the garden out back. I think it will be to your liking."

"Thank you," Miriam said with a warm smile. "I'm sure it will."

"If you need anything else, I—"

"Don't prattle on, Mary," Mark's butler, Asher, admonished as he came into the entryway. "I'm sure Mr. and Mrs. Bennett would like some time alone. I have champagne ready for you in the parlor, along with some appetizers before supper."

"Are you hungry?" Mark asked, gesturing towards the hall behind him. "Cook should have supper ready for us in just a bit, but in the meantime, we can drink to our new life."

"I'm actually quite exhausted from my trip. Do you mind if I retire for the evening?"

Mark hid his disappointment as he nodded. "Of course, if you change your mind, just ring for one of the servants and one of them will bring you up a plate of food."

"I'll take you to your room, now, Mrs. Bennett,"

Mary offered as they made their way over to the staircase.

As Mark watched his wife glide up the stairs, he wondered what he'd gotten himself into. A wife in theory was one thing, but now he had one living under his own roof. Did he make the right decision, or was he going to live to regret his choice?

7

The next morning, Miriam woke to the chirping sound of birds outside. She stretched her arms above her head, before standing up and moving over to the window. There was a nest filled with a family of bluebirds and the mother was busy feeding her chicks. It caused Miriam to think of her own youngling, and she placed her hand on her belly

When would be the right time to tell Mark about the baby? Should she do it like a bandage, and rip it off right away, or would it be better to build up a relationship with him before she broke the news? If she wanted a positive outcome, she needed to make herself indispensable in Mark's life.

It was her only hope for making their marriage work.

She let out a heavy sigh as she leaned against the window frame. A chill crawled up her spine, causing her to shiver. She wished she had a robe to put on over her slip, but that was another luxury she didn't have the money for.

She opened her wardrobe, prepared to wear her dirty outfit from the previous day. To her surprise, both of her dresses were inside, freshly cleaned and pressed, along with her undergarments folded on the bottom shelf. The rip in her yellow dress had even been mended. Had Mary done all of this for her? Tears filled her eyes, touched by the kind gesture. She was used to servants doing tasks for her, but it was out of fear from the imperial family. Mary made her feel like family.

Miriam slipped on the yellow dress and made quick work of putting her hair up in a bun. She pinched her cheeks to give them color, then headed downstairs, hoping it wasn't too late for breakfast. Skipping dinner the previous night had left her famished.

After poking her head into several wrong rooms downstairs, she finally found the dining room. Mark was sitting at the head of the table, reading a newspaper as he sipped on a cup of coffee. His eyes peeked over the edge of the paper and settled on her.

"I'm sure you're hungry. Why don't you have a seat." Mark gestured to the chair next to him. "Cook made pancakes as well as fried bacon and poached eggs. There's also some fresh fruit and toasted bread if you'd rather have that."

"Thank you." Miriam took the offered seat and helped herself to some of the fruit as well as the eggs. She figured it would be the easiest on her stomach. She poured herself a cup of coffee, taking a long swig before setting it down. "After we eat, what are our plans for the day?"

"I have to head over to the mine, so you're free to do whatever you like until I return tonight and we head over to my family's house for supper."

Miriam wasn't sure what to make of his suggestion. She hoped he would take the day off and help her settle into her new life.

"Is there anything you need me to do?"

He shrugged, folding the paper back up. "Not that I can think of. You mentioned only having a pair of dresses. If you'd like, you could have Hucksley—my driver—take you into Yuma to purchase some new clothes."

"Wouldn't you want to approve what I buy?" she asked in astonishment, knowing that her former husband controlled every aspect of her life, including her wardrobe.

Mark's brows furrowed together in confusion as he placed the paper down beside him. "I don't see a need for that. I have an account at the dress shop from when my sister used to live with me before she got married. Just tell them you're my new wife, and they'll get you whatever you need."

Miriam swallowed a couple of times, trying to process that not only was he giving her free rein to pick out her own clothes, but it seemed there was no limit to what she could purchase. "You're certain about this? Whatever I need?"

He nodded. "Enjoy yourself, Miriam. You're never going to have to worry about money again." He stood from his chair and headed towards the door. "Oh, and make sure to pick up a bouquet of fresh flowers for my aunt and some cigars for my uncle. Arriving with gifts will make our news a bit more palatable."

"I'll make sure to do that." Miriam needed every ounce of help she could get. The last thing she wanted to do was get off on the wrong foot with her new husband's family. Two hours later, she arrived at the dress shop, ready to pick out the ideal dress to make the perfect first impression.

"What can I do for you?" the dress shop owner asked with a forced smile, as she looked Miriam up and down with a skeptical eye.

"I need to purchase a few dresses, as well as a couple of skirts and blouses."

The woman glanced down at her attire, a doubtful look settling on her face. "Do you have enough money with you to cover that? We don't allow purchases on credit."

Miriam knew the woman was judging her based off of her current outfit. What she wouldn't give to have one of her old dresses from the imperial court. This woman wouldn't have dared to treat her this way if she had one of those gowns on. "I hate to have to return home and tell my husband that you wouldn't let me put the items on his account."

"And who is your husband, may I ask?" the woman inquired with a disbelieving tone as she placed her hand on her hip with a superior attitude.

"Mr. Mark Bennett. We were just married yesterday," Miriam explained. "He insisted I come to your store and that you would take good care of me."

The other woman's shoulders curled over her

chest as her face flushed with embarrassment. "Please forgive me, Mrs. Bennett," she stammered out.` "I had no idea who you were. Anything you want, it's yours. If I don't have something, I'll have it shipped from New York or Paris just for you."

Miriam spent the next three hours picking out a half a dozen dresses and gowns, three skirts with complimentary blouses, as well as two pairs of boots, and matching hats, and a robe to complete her new wardrobe.

She picked out the satin plum gown to wear home, adding a pair of black boots and matching hat to finish her ensemble.

"What would you like me to do with your old dress?" the store owner asked.

"You can donate it to charity," she ordered, grateful to be free of the dress that was truthfully little more than a rag. It had served its purpose by getting her to her new life, but now it was time to leave it in the past with everything else she wanted to forget.

Miriam arrived back at the Bennett house, and the driver delivered all of her packages inside. Mary and Tandy busied themselves putting away the items, gushing over each one and telling Miriam what exceptional taste she had.

"You're going to look mighty pretty on Mr. Bennett's arm in these clothes. Even Miss Becca doesn't have these nice of outfits," Tandy pointed out, her youthful exuberance splashed across her face.

"Hush now, girl, it's not your job to comment on Mrs. Bennett's choices," Mary reprimanded the younger maid.

"Did I overdo it, Mary? I don't want to look pretentious?" Miriam asked with concern as she sat in her chair next to them. She was used to picking out clothes to impress people in the imperial court; would her sense of style be as appreciated here in the West?

Mary shook her head. "No, ma'am, they're just right for the wife of the largest copper mine owner in all of Arizona."

Miriam nearly choked on the tea she was drinking when she heard the new information. She had no idea that Mark's copper mine was that large. From his advert, it had been clear he had means, but not on that massive of a scale. No wonder he promised her she'd never have to worry about money again.

The tea and cookies weren't settling right with Miriam, and the room started to sway. It had to be the baby making her sick again. She rushed over to her bed, and laid down.

"Are you all right, Mrs. Bennett?" she heard Mary inquire from across the room. "Do I need to send someone to fetch Mr. Bennett?"

"No, Mary, I just need to rest," she sputtered out with trepidation. "I'm still recovering from my trip. Can you wake me up in an hour so I can get ready for this evening?"

"Yes, ma'am, I'll just let you rest, and I'll be back in a bit."

What was going to happen when a bout of sickness happened when Mark was present? She could only blame her trip for so long before he figured out something else was going on. Soon, it was going to become impossible for her to hide her condition. She needed to tell her husband before that time came. Silently, she sent up a prayer before she drifted off to sleep, asking God to help her in her situation.

True to her word, Mary woke her an hour later, and helped her get ready for the dinner party. Miriam made her way downstairs and picked out a book to read while she waited for Mark to return home.

She was twenty pages into the story when he

entered the parlor. He was wearing his same brown suit from earlier, which had prompted her to pick out a sapphire blue gown that would complement it.

His eyes widened with appreciation. "I see my money was well spent today. You look stunning in that gown."

She could feel her cheeks tinge pink from the compliment. "Thank you. It feels nice to be wearing a fine garment like this again." Realizing the statement hinted at more than she wanted to reveal about her past, she quickly changed the subject by adding, "I got everything you requested for your family. The items are waiting in the foyer."

"Excellent; are you ready to leave then?"

She nodded as she placed the book on the table in front of her.

"What were you reading?" he inquired with curiosity as he moved over and glanced at the title "Shakespeare—interesting choice."

"What can I say, I'm a hopeless romantic at heart."

"Join the club," he teased with a wink. "It's probably why I waited so long to get married. I kept holding out hope that I'd just randomly bump into the woman of my dreams."

"How did that work out for you," she teased back. "You ended up with a mail order bride instead."

"It doesn't mean she couldn't end up being the woman of my dreams," he pointed out, coming to sit beside her. "Sometimes things happen in the most unexpected ways."

He leaned towards her, the nearness of him almost more than she could bear. She could tell he wanted to kiss her, but she wasn't ready for that yet. Purposely wanting to diffuse the situation, she scooted away from him and blurted out, "I have a dreadful joke for you."

"You do? Okay, let's hear it." Mark leaned back against the couch, placing his hands behind his head, taking the cue that she needed space between them.

"Who is the greatest chicken-killer in Shakespeare?"

"I have no idea."

"Macbeth, because he did murder most foul."

There was a long pause before Mark chuckled, slapping his knee. "You're right; that is rather dreadful, but I love it."

"Good, I've got plenty more where that came from."

"Is that so? Why don't you keep them coming then?"

She shook her head. "What would be the fun in that? It's better to sprinkle them in when you least expect them."

"You're going to keep me guessing, aren't you?"

She let out a laugh, causing her face to scrunch up with amusement. "Don't we need to be going? We don't want to keep your family waiting."

He nodded, standing up and reaching out his hand to her. "Come on, let's get this over with."

8

As Mark escorted Miriam into his sister's house, he braced himself for the barrage of questions that were sure to follow once they heard the news of his marriage.

"Are you ready for this?" he asked, looking over at Miriam as his hand hovered over the door handle to the dining room.

"As much as I can be," she stated, squeezing her hands together in front of her. "I hope they like me."

"You're an easy person to like," Mark assured her. "You have nothing to worry about."

She seemed to relax, her hands falling to her side as a small smile formed on her lips.

Mark pushed open the doors to reveal his sister, Becca, and her husband, Garrett, sitting at the head of the table. His cousin, Julia, and her husband, Ed, were on one side with his Aunt Claire sitting across, and at the other end of the table, was his Uncle Martin.

The conversation stopped abruptly and all eyes turned to focus on them. Becca stood from her seat and walked over to the newlyweds. "I'm so glad you're here."

She guided them over to the table and gestured to the empty seats. "Please, join us."

"Shouldn't there be introductions first?" Mark heard his uncle ask in a huff. "I'm not accustomed to eating with strangers. After all, this is a family dinner; I have no idea why my nephew thought it appropriate to bring a guest."

"She isn't a guest, Uncle Martin; she *is* family," Mark corrected. "I hoped to do this in a different way, but it seems I'm left with no other option. Everyone, this is my wife, Miriam."

"Wife?" his aunt gasped out, her hand flying up to cover her mouth. "I must be mishearing things, because I would swear you just announced that you're married."

"You didn't mishear anything, Aunt Claire. I am a married man as of yesterday," Mark reiterated. "Becca can confirm the fact. She was present for the ceremony at the church."

"You were there?" Julia accused with anger written across her face. "Why didn't you tell me, Becca? We tell each other everything."

"It wasn't my secret to divulge—my brother wanted to be the one to tell everyone," Becca defended herself. "And now that he has, we should all support him in his decision and welcome Miriam into the family."

"I just don't understand," Aunt Claire whined as she tapped the side of her wine glass. "I had several perfectly wonderful candidates for you to marry right here in Little Ridge and Yuma. Why would you go out of your way to find someone else?"

"Because I want to be in control of my own life. You think you know what I want in a partner, but you don't. When Miriam answered my advert, I knew she was exactly what I wanted in a wife."

"An advert?" Uncle Martin, Aunt Claire, and Julia all blurted out at the same time.

"You can't be serious. Did you actually place

one of those awful mail order bride adverts in the newspaper?" Aunt Claire questioned in shock.

Uncle Martin slammed his glass down on the table, glaring at Mark. "Do you know what will happen to this family's reputation once everyone finds out? We're going to be the joke of Little Ridge."

"How could you be so selfish, Mark?" Julia whispered in disbelief. "To not only do something so harmful to the family, but to do it behind our backs. I thought you were better than this." Then turning her attention to her other cousin, she added, "And you, Becca, I understand that he's your brother, but how can you be okay with this? Why would you support him in such folly?"

"Because he is my brother, and even when he didn't agree with my choice to be with Garrett, he supported me. I owe him the same loyalty; we both do since he supported your decision to be matched with Ed, despite your husband's past exploits."

Julia slowly nodded, the anger dissipating from her as she relaxed into her seat. "You're right, Becca. I shouldn't pass judgment on Mark and his new wife."

"Thank you for that Julia; as for you Aunt Claire

and Uncle Martin, you both might be upset and not understand my choice, but I can assure you, it was the right one. Once you get to know Miriam, you'll see she's wonderful; she's smart, funny, and kind-hearted." Mark reached out and squeezed his wife's hand. "I hope you will give her a chance, but if you won't, then you'll be choosing to cut me out of your life as well."

The patriarch and matriarch of the Bennett family sat stunned for several seconds before Uncle Martin finally broke the silence. "You are my only nephew, and your brother meant a great deal to me. I could never turn my back on you."

"And as for Miriam? Will you treat her with the respect she deserves as my wife?"

"I will do my best."

"And how about you, Aunt Claire? Can you treat Miriam as part of the family?"

Aunt Claire stood from her chair and marched over to Mark and Miriam. For a moment, he was afraid his aunt was going to make a scene. Instead, she reached out and pulled Miriam into a hug. "I can't help myself; I'm incapable of staying mad for very long. Of course, I'll welcome Miriam into the family." She pulled back and gave them both a smile. "I think your marriage calls for a toast."

The standing members of the family took their

seats around the table as one of the servants came into the room and poured everyone a glass of champagne.

Ed stood to his feet and raised his glass in the air. "Let me do the honors. To the bride and groom, may your happiness be as deep as the sea and your troubles as light as its foam."

Aunt Claire spent the next hour giving them guidance as they ate dinner. "The best advice I can give you is to make laughter the score of your marriage. Even in difficult times, you need to find a reason to laugh."

"That's not a problem, Aunt Claire; we agreed to laugh at each other's jokes, even the most dreadful of ones."

"I'm glad to hear that," she said, giving an approving smile to both of them. "There's no point in taking life too seriously. Always leave room for amusement."

"And just remember, there isn't such a thing as a perfect marriage, just two imperfect people who agree to never give up on each other," Garrett added. "Becca never gave up on me, and that's the reason we're happily married."

"All of that advice is good and well, but I think we should be focusing on making Miriam feel welcome. Has Mark given you a tour around town?" Becca inquired after taking a sip of her champagne.

Miriam shook her head. "He's been busy at the mine, and I needed to go into Yuma to run some errands anyway."

"Yuma? Why would you send her there?" Becca inquired with confusion. "Most anything she would need she could get in Little Ridge."

Mark shifted in his seat, uncomfortable that his sister would draw attention to the fact he'd sent his new wife to the neighboring city to shop. Part of him had done it to keep the townsfolk from prying into who she was, but another part did it to provide her with better options. "The dress shop in Yuma is far superior to the minuscule offerings at the mercantile. Since she needed several items, I thought it best if she went into Yuma."

"Why did you need new clothes?" Julia probed with an arched eyebrow. "Didn't you bring your belongings with you?"

"I didn't have much I could bring," Miriam confessed as a flush creeped across her cheeks. "Mark was kind enough to offer to buy me a few outfits."

"And so it begins," Uncle Martin sighed. "I

hope you're ready for a life of having to always provide more and more for a wife that never seems to be happy with what you give her."

"Father, you shouldn't say such things," Julia softly scolded. "Mother wasn't like that."

"Julia, you were quite young when your mother passed away, and I shielded you from her less-than desirable attributes. For the most part, she was a wonderful woman, but she had an unquenchable thirst for material possessions, as do most women," Uncle Martin stated pointedly as he glared at Miriam.

"It wasn't like that. I was content to wear my own dresses," Miriam explained as her eyes fell to the table.

Mark jumped to her defense. "It was all my idea; I wanted her to make a good impression tonight and I thought a new dress could go a long way in that regard."

"I'm not feeling well. Can we leave, please," Miriam requested in a whisper.

"Look at what you've all done; you've upset my wife only one day after our wedding. I brought her here because I trusted my family to be civil to her, but even that was impossible." Mark jerked up from the table and threw his napkin down. He stretched out his arm and offered his hand to his wife. "Let's get out of here."

Just before they reached the front door, Becca came rushing up to them, grabbing her brother by the arm to stop him. "Please wait; I have something I need to say."

"I'm really not in the mood, Becca," Mark objected. "I think enough has been said tonight to last us a lifetime."

"I know some hurtful things were said tonight, but none of them were by me. I've done nothing but welcome Miriam into my home and treat her like a sister."

"She's right, Mark," Miriam agreed. "Your sister isn't to blame for what happened tonight. I don't know what we were expecting to happen, ambushing them all the way we did. You should have talked with them first before introducing me to them."

"Just give Uncle Martin some time to adjust—he's never done well with surprises. The rest of the family seems to be accepting the news in stride, once the shock wore off. In the meantime, I'm going to do what my brother should have done when you first got here. I'm going to show you around town tomorrow."

"That's very kind of you, but you don't have to do that," Miriam said. "I don't want to cause any problems for you with your uncle."

"Don't worry about that. You're my sister now, and I want to make you feel at home here in Little Ridge. I'm not taking 'no' for an answer, so I'll be at your house in the morning at ten a.m. to fetch you."

9

After a restless night of sleep wondering what she could have done differently to make Mark's uncle approve of her, Miriam woke up feeling defeated. She had a good mind to roll back over and close her eyes to shut out how much had gone wrong since her arrival in Little Ridge. On top of Mark's family being less than enthused about her entrance into their family, she still hadn't had a chance to tell Mark about her pregnancy. She figured after the failure of the dinner last night, she couldn't very well blurt out that she was with child from her previous marriage. She needed to find a way to make everything better with his family before she revealed the truth.

"Mrs. Bennett, you told me to wake you in the

morning so you could get ready for your outing with Mrs. Casner."

Miriam sat up and leaned back against the headrest of her bed. "Thank you, Mary, but I'm not sure I'm going today."

"It isn't good for you to lay in this room all day. You should spend the day with Mrs. Casner. She'll surely lift your spirits. I raised her since she was a wee babe, and she's got a heart of gold."

Miriam knew Mary was right. Spending the day in bed wasn't going to do her any good. If she wanted to find a solution to her problems, she needed to do something about them. If she got to know Becca, perhaps she could ask for help with the rest of the family.

"I think I will wear my lavender dress with the lace accents." Miriam sat up and swung her legs over the side of the bed. "I want to make a good impression when I meet people around town."

"I'll get it out for you right now, Mrs. Bennett." Mary rushed over and opened the wardrobe, pulling out the requested dress, then helped Miriam get ready.

As Mary secured the dress around her, she wondered how long before her body betrayed her, and revealed that she was pregnant. She purposely got her new dresses slightly bigger than she needed, but they would only last so long before her secret couldn't be hidden anymore. She couldn't help but feel like there was an hourglass running out on her.

By the time she went down for breakfast, Miriam was ready to work towards making her situation better. When she found a note from her husband waiting by her breakfast, it lifted her spirits to know he was thinking of her.

IN AN EFFORT TO cheer you up, I thought I would tell you a dreadful joke.

A LADY WROTE the following letters at the bottom of her flour barrel:

O I C U R M T

PLEASE TRY to enjoy your time with my sister. Don't worry about anything besides settling in to your new life here in Little Ridge.

YOUR HUSBAND,

Mark

SHE FOLDED up the letter and put it in her reticule, wanting to keep it to remind herself that she wasn't in this alone. The more she got to know Mark, the more she realized he was the exact opposite of her first husband. He cared about her wants and needs, defended her to others including his own family, and he didn't demonstrate a mean bone in his body. She wanted to believe that if she told him about the baby, he would understand, but part of her worried it would be too much for him to handle. Accepting another man's baby as his own was a lot to ask anyone, even a man as good as Mark Bennett was proving to be.

Just as Becca promised, she arrived at the house promptly at ten a.m. with a giant grin spread across her face. "Good morning, Miriam, are you ready to get to know your new town?"

"I have to admit, I'm a bit nervous. Little Ridge is quite different from where I grew up in Russia. I don't know if I'm going to fit in here."

"You're going to find that the townsfolk are wonderful. They might be a bit nosy and ask one-too-many questions, but they mean well."

Miriam stiffened at the thought of having to deflect questions about her past all day. Becca hadn't made an issue of it, and she had hoped her luck would continue with everyone else she met in Little Ridge. From what her new sister-in-law was telling her, she wasn't going to have such luck.

"I thought the first place we could stop off is at the apothecary where you can meet one of my dearest friends, June Wentworth," Becca explained as they headed out of the house and towards Main Street. "I think you'll find that you have a lot in common with her. She just moved back to town last year after living in Yuma with her first husband for a few years. She's a widow, who just recently married her old beau. They just had a baby, and she also has a son from her first marriage."

"How did her husband take to the idea of raising another man's baby?" Miriam probed. "That couldn't have been easy."

"Daniel loved June, and her son came with her as part of the deal."

"So he accepted her son so he could be with her?" Miriam inquired with interest. She wondered, if she could make her husband fall in love with her, would he be willing to accept her son as his own?

"It was more than that; he cares about Ben, and

he is as much of a father to him as he is their daughter."

June and Daniel's situation gave Miriam hope that her own husband might be able to care for her child as his own; at least, if she were able to get him to love her. If he wasn't invested in Miriam, it would be far too easy for him to be able to turn them away. She couldn't risk telling him until she was certain he wouldn't do that. Both her life and that of her unborn child's depended on it.

Becca stopped in front of a simple wooden building with the word, 'Apothecary' painted on a sign hung above the door. "We're here."

The small building housed several wooden display counters with glass tops, which held various bottles and containers filled with tonics and powders used to heal various ailments. A pretty brown-haired woman stood behind the counter towards the back. She waved them over, saying, "I'm so glad you're here, Becca." Then glancing at Miriam, she added, "And who do you have with you?"

"This is Miriam Bennett, my brother's new wife," Becca explained. "And before you ask, you didn't receive an invite because it was a small wedding."

It was clear from the skeptical look on her face, June had more questions she wanted to ask. To Miriam's relief, she didn't voice them. Instead, she greeted her with a warm smile. "It's nice to meet you, Miriam. My husband, Daniel, is good friends with Mark. I'm sure he'll be glad to hear he's finally settled down, as I am. Mark's been alone for far too long."

"Is there a reason for that?" Miriam inquired, but quickly regretted it when both women glanced away. "I'm sorry, I should probably ask my husband that rather than either of you."

"It's okay. He'd probably avoid answering the question, anyway," Becca said, patting Miriam's hand that rested on the counter. "Between you and me, he spends way too much time at the mine. Ever since our parents died, it's like he's determined to prove that he can do the job every bit as well as our father did."

Miriam didn't expect to hear that, though it wasn't surprising. Mark had been at the mine all day yesterday and had gone there first thing this morning. The pattern was clear and she wasn't sure what to do about it. She'd already spent a year married to a man that made bad choices because he lived in the shadow of his father. She didn't want to have a repeat of the same situation. Could she help him let go of his obsession of being at the mine for long hours at a time? Was there some way she could show Mark there was more to life than work?

The women chatted about several town events coming up, as well as the fiasco of a baptism when the Johnson boy panicked in the water the previous Sunday. By the time they were ready to leave, Miriam felt like for the first time in her life, she might have a chance to make real friends. That was, if everything worked out with Mark after she told him about the baby.

The baby. What would her new friends think once they found out that she was carrying another man's child? Even though it was her previous husband's baby, it didn't make it Mark's. Would they look at her differently because of it? Was it better if she didn't invest in them just in case they reacted poorly to the news once it came out?

"I was curious about the mercantile and what they offer. Do you mind taking me there next?" Miriam asked, wanting to remove herself from June's presence before she let herself invest anymore in the other woman.

"It was nice meeting you, Miriam. Make sure to not be a stranger, and stop by any time," June offered with a smile. "And you should come to the women's auxiliary meeting this Friday night. We're planning the town's next social."

"I'll have to think about it," Miriam said, unwilling to commit to attending.

"Well, the offer isn't going anywhere. You're always welcome."

Becca and Miriam exited the apothecary and made their way through the rest of Main Street. On their way to the mercantile, Becca pointed out the saloon and the boarding house. When they entered the general store that supplied the entire town with essential items, Becca introduced her to the owner as well as the post master who ran the post office next door. After that, Becca introduced her to Dr. Billford, the town doctor. Their final stop for the day was the Copper Café, where they enjoyed a midday meal.

Mr. Walker, who owned and ran the local newspaper, stopped by their table, eager to meet the newest resident of the town. "I'd love to interview you and feature your story on the front page of the paper," he offered.

"No, that won't be necessary," Miriam cried out, her voice shaking with fear. The last thing she needed was for her picture to be published in a newspaper and then end up in the wrong hands. Wanting to squash the idea, she quickly added, "I led a rather dull life back in Russia. I assure you, there's nothing of interest."

"Well, if you change your mind, you can visit me at my office at the end of Main Street."

"What was that all about? Why didn't you want Mr. Walker to feature you in the newspaper?" Becca probed.

Miriam shrugged, averting her eyes in an effort to hide how uncomfortable the topic was making her. "Like I told Mr. Walker, there's nothing worth printing about my life."

"It seems to me, you're afraid of something. Are you embarrassed about something from your past?"

Miriam picked up her glass of lemonade and took a long sip, trying to figure out the right way to answer Becca without revealing anything that would expose the truth. "I don't like talking about it, but my first husband was an awful, vile man who didn't have a drop of loyalty or trustworthiness in his body. I told Mark as such, but if I never have to speak of him again, it would make me happy."

Becca reached across the table and patted her hand. "Say no more. I will never bring it up again."

Later that afternoon, Miriam set to work to

figure out a way to make herself invaluable to her husband. Once he depended on her, perhaps that could turn into love. Her first stop was in the kitchen, but the cook immediately ushered her out, explaining that the mistress of the house had no business being in there. She asked Mary if there was anything she could do around the house, but the woman politely declined, explaining that she'd taken care of the house for over two decades, and didn't need anyone disrupting her cleaning routine with Tandy. Miriam had the same results with the groundskeeper and the butler, reminding her of how useless she felt back in Russia. She might have been a princess, but the title held little real power. It seemed she was to have the same fate in America, playing the part of Mark Bennett's insipid wife.

Frustrated, Miriam returned to her room, deciding that at a bare minimum, she could at least make herself appealing to him for when he returned home from the mine. After quizzing Tandy about her husband's preferences, she picked out an emerald green gown and placed her hair half-up with curls coming down around her neck. She added a touch of rouge to her cheeks, then headed downstairs to wait for his arrival.

Hours ticked by, and when he finally did return,

she was nearly falling asleep in her chair at the dining room table.

"You waited up for me?" he asked in astonishment. "You shouldn't have bothered."

Miriam held back the sigh, as well as the accusatory words, that wanted to fall from her lips. The last thing she needed to do was make him feel bad about his late homecoming. Such an outburst would set back her plan, and she couldn't afford for that to happen.

Instead, she plastered on her most endearing smile and stood from her chair. She walked over and removed the cover from the plate of food. "It wasn't a bother. I had Cook set this aside for you, as well as a plate for myself."

"You didn't have to go to all this trouble. I'm used to eating my meals by myself."

"That might be true, but it doesn't have to be the case anymore. You have a wife now, that wants to spend time with you."

"What's going on, Miriam? Why are you pushing this issue?" Mark asked in a confused tone.

"All I want to do is make you happy," she mewled in frustration. "What is it going to take to make you want to spend time with me?"

"It's not that I don't want to spend time with

you, but I'm right in the middle of the final preparation for the expansion at the mine."

"I don't know much about mining, but as the owner, don't you have people that work for you that can handle that?"

"I do, but I've learned over the years, that no one takes care of your business the way you do yourself. I have to make sure this expansion happens without any complications."

Miriam nodded, hating the answer, but knowing from the firm tone in his voice, she wasn't going to be able to change his mind. "At least sit down for supper," she suggested as she gestured to the table. "You can tell me about the expansion while we eat."

Mark took a seat and pulled the plate of food towards him. "You want to hear about that?"

"Does that surprise you?" she asked in return as she sat across form him.

"My mother never cared about hearing about the mine. Sure, she enjoyed the income from it, but she preferred to spend her days at social gatherings or church bazaars."

"Is that all you expect of me? Am I to be nothing more than a vapid debutante who spends her days floating from one event to another?"

"No, that's not what I'm saying. I'm not sure why you're upset; most women would love to have nothing to worry about except what dress to wear for a party."

Miriam couldn't help herself. She wanted to endear Mark to herself, but she'd already spent the first half of her life playing the part of a noble-woman, then a princess. The idea of spending the rest of her life doing the same was more than she could bear. She came to America to start over, not find herself trapped in the same life she escaped in Russia.

"Now that you've made it clear what you expect of me, I think I will retire for the evening." Miriam stood from the table and started to leave.

Mark reached out and stopped her. "I thought you were going to eat with me."

"Do you want me to?" she probed, hoping there might be a bit of hope after all.

He nodded. "I didn't mean to upset you, Miriam. I'm sorry. If you could give me a little grace, I'd appreciate it. I'm new to being a husband."

The tension in her receded, and instead, a tingling sensation replaced it. Warmth spread up her arm from where his hand rested on her wrist.

Her eyes moved down to his, and for a moment, she could swear she saw desire reflected in them.

He pulled his hand away and his gaze darted to the table as he gestured towards the chair she'd just vacated. "Please eat; you must be famished."

Miriam did as he requested. They spent the meal discussing the mine as well as the women's auxiliary and knitting club. By the end of the meal, she felt like she understood his business more, and she'd agreed to make an effort to participate in local activities.

As they headed upstairs to go to bed, Miriam realized that though it wasn't in the way she expected, she'd managed to grow closer to Mark. She just hoped that by the time she had to tell him about the baby, he would care enough about her that he wouldn't be able to let her go.

10

Three weeks passed by, and Mark and Miriam were finding a natural rhythm to their life together. Because of his wife's encouragement, he was spending less time at the mine and more time at home with her. What surprised him about the change was that he enjoyed spending time with her more than working. She had a fascinating mind—her complex thoughts rivaled his own—making discussions about the books they were reading engaging. She was also quick-witted and observant, finding humor in situations that he himself, often didn't notice.

Today, on his way home from work, he had stopped by the general store to pick up a surprise for his wife. He'd ordered a new book for her and couldn't wait to surprise her with it.

Once home, he made a beeline straight for the parlor, expecting to find Miriam reading on the divan by the window; however, she wasn't there. He rang the bell and a few moments later, Tandy came rushing into the room. "What can I do for you, Mr. Bennett?" the young woman asked as she came to stand in front of him.

"Where is my wife?"

"She wasn't feeling well this afternoon, and retired to her room."

"That's been happening a lot lately," Mark observed to himself, concern for her causing him to ponder what might be wrong with her constitution to cause such a regular sickness. "I think I will go check on her."

"No, don't do that," Tandy burst out, her eyes widening with apprehension. "You'll surely wake Mrs. Bennett; she was sleeping when last I checked on her."

"Tandy, I appreciate your concern for my wife's need for rest, but I want to see for myself that she's feeling better."

Mark marched up the stairs and made his way to the rose room. He softly tapped on the door.

When he didn't hear a response, he twisted the knob and pushed the door open. Just as Tandy described, Miriam was sleeping in her bed with the drapes firmly shut to drown out the light. She looked so peaceful—like a serene angel—laying there, he couldn't help but move closer to watch her.

The floor creaked beneath his feet, causing Miriam's eyelids to flutter. "No, no, not tonight. Please, not again. I promise, I'll do exactly what you ask," she whimpered out, as she thrashed back and forth in her bed.

Mark's heart broke, realizing that she must be mistaking him for her deceased husband. What had that man done to her to make her react so? She'd mentioned in her letter that he was a rotten man, but it seemed well beyond that. Had he beaten her, forced himself on her? The thought of it made Mark seethe with anger. Miriam was the most wonderful woman in the world, and deserved to be treated like a queen, not mistreated and abused. Instantly, he made the resolution to himself, that no matter what, he was going to do right by her.

"It's all right, Miriam, you have nothing to worry about as long as you are with me," Mark coaxed as he knelt down beside her bed and placed his hand on her arm. "I won't let anything bad happen to you."

Miriam's eyes flew open and she sat up, jerking her arm away from Mark. "What, what's going on?" Her eyes darted around the room, as if in a panic, then finally settled on Mark. Slowly, her terror subsided and she leaned back against the headrest of the bed.

"I think you were having a bad dream. Do you want to talk about it?" Mark inquired, hoping that he'd built up enough rapport with her that she felt like she could trust him.

Miriam shook her head. "It was nothing."

"Are you sure? It didn't look like nothing. You can trust me, Miriam. I'm not like your first husband. I'll never hurt you."

She lifted her hands up, palms towards Mark. "I don't want to talk about it. All of that is in my past. I just want to start over with you."

"But from the way you just reacted, it's not in the past, Miriam—not really. Why won't you let me in? Why won't you tell me what is going on with you?"

She scooted away from him and jumped up from the other side of the bed. "Why can't you leave my past in the past? Can't you see, it's too painful for me to talk about." She grabbed the robe from the nearby chair and threw it on. "If you will excuse me, I need to visit the privy." She headed towards the door that led to the other room, but before she could get away, Mark reached out to stop her.

"Miriam, what is going on? Please, tell me," he begged, wanting to understand the reason as to why even though they had grown close intellectually and emotionally, there was still a distinct distance between them physically.

"I can't," she sputtered out, trying to pull away. "You won't understand."

"No, don't just run away because it's easier. I know you're attracted to me. I can see it in your eyes when we're alone—I can see it in them right now. Something is holding you back." He pulled her close against him until their bodies were pressed up against one another. "I want to know every part of you, Miriam, even the hidden ones."

For a moment, he thought she might actually let him kiss her, but something so unexpected happened, he nearly fell over from shock. A sharp jab, almost like a kick, thrust out at him. His eyes darted down to her belly, and through her robe, he could tell it was sticking out further than it had when she first arrived in Arizona.

"What's going on with your stomach, Miriam? Is there something you need to tell me?" Even as he asked the words, he knew the answer. It all made sense now—why she had been acting so distant, why it felt like she had a secret she was hiding. It was about her first husband, but not what Mark had speculated. "You need to tell me right now, Miriam. Are you pregnant?"

Her eyes welled up with tears and she jerked back in dismay. "Why did you have to get so close to me? I didn't want you to find out this way."

"So, it's true, then; you're carrying another man's child?" Mark asked in astonishment.

"I'd planned to tell you after church tomorrow, but now everything is ruined," she cried out in despair. "You must hate me for keeping this from you."

"When did you know?" he accused. "Did you know when you responded to my advert?"

Miriam shook her head. "No, I only found out when I was traveling here to marry you."

"But you kept it from me, and married me anyway, knowing that your condition could change my mind about our agreement?"

"It wasn't like that," Miriam defended, reaching out and placing her hand on his arm. "I tried to tell you at the church, but your sister interrupted us before I could. Then everything happened so fast, there was never another chance."

"What about after we were married? You had countless times when you could have told me. What made you keep all of this from me?"

Miriam started to shake, sobs pouring from her to the point he knew she could faint at any moment. He guided her over to the nearby chair, then helped her into it, then took a seat in the one beside it.

"I almost told you so many times, but I was afraid of what you would do when you found out. I have nowhere else to go, no way of taking care of myself or the baby. I hoped, over time, you would come to care enough for me to accept my baby as your own."

Mark sagged back against the chair, shocked by the news. What did this mean for him, for them? Could he do what she asked? Did he have it in him to love another man's child as his own?

"What are you going to do now that you know? Are you going to toss us out?" Miriam inquired, the fear clear in her voice as her hand moved to rest on her belly in a defensive manner.

"Of course not; I would never do that to a pregnant woman."

"Does that mean you're willing to be a family with us?"

He could hear the hope in her voice, and part of him wanted to alleviate her fear by agreeing right on the spot, but he knew that wouldn't be right if he couldn't stick to the promise. "I need time to think and pray about this. The baby changes everything."

Mark stood up from the chair and exited the room, knowing that if he stayed with her a moment longer, he might give in to her request because of how much he cared for her. The problem was, there was more than just how he felt about Miriam to consider. What would the people around town, or the men at the mine say, once the news came out? What would his family think? Had they been right about placing the mail order bride advert? Did this turn of events prove he'd been stupid and reckless to do such a thing?

Without realizing it, he found himself standing outside the church. He made his way around to the back and knocked on the door that led to Pastor Murphy's office.

"Good afternoon, Mr. Bennett," the pastor

greeted, as he ushered Mark inside and walked him over to a set of chairs by his desk. "What can I do for you?"

"I was hoping you might have a bit of time to talk with me about a situation with my wife."

"Of course; I know adjusting to marriage can be difficult. What's going on?"

"I hate to say this, but this goes beyond simple newlywed problems. I found out today that my wife is pregnant."

"Well, congratulations. That's rather fast, but if God sees fit to give you a baby this quickly, you should be happy about it."

"I would be, if the baby was mine. As it turns out, she's carrying the baby of her deceased husband," Mark lamented. "And I don't know what to do about it."

"Did she lie to you about it when she agreed to marry you?"

Mark shook his head. "She told me she didn't know until she was already traveling to marry me. I want to believe her; I mean, she's never done anything to make me think she's dishonest. Well, at least, until now."

"Did she give you a reason why she didn't tell you when she got here, or after you were married?"

"Yes, she was afraid what I would do when I found out."

"Mr. Bennett, I know this is an incredibly difficult situation. Many men would think to end the marriage on grounds of fraud because they were too weak to handle taking on another man's baby. I think you're better than that though. From all the years I've known you, you've always been an honorable and good man."

"How do I do this, Pastor Murphy? I'm not sure I can handle taking this on. It feels like too much," Mark confessed.

"Marriage is a commitment, not a feeling. You promised Miriam to be her husband, and you can't take that back simply because something has happened that you didn't expect. The hardest part of a marriage is not giving up when things get tough."

"You're right. I made a commitment and I need to honor that."

"Let me pray with you before you go."

A half hour later, Mark arrived back at his house, ready to tell Miriam of his decision. He found her sitting in the parlor, reading a book. She set the book down on the table, her eyes probing him for any clues to what he was thinking. "Have you made a decision about what you're going to do?"

"I made a commitment to you when I married you, and I plan on keeping it. I'll claim your baby as my own."

"You will?" she gushed with relief. "I was so afraid, Mark. I've come to care so much for you, that the thought of losing you was frightening. I'm sorry for breaking your trust, but I will do whatever it takes to earn it back."

He nodded, reaching out to take her hand. "I forgive you, Miriam. You were in a tough situation and you did the best you could. Everything is going to be fine now that I know what you were keeping from me."

Miriam's eyes flickered away for a moment before they returned to him, and a smile emerged. "You're right; now that you know about the baby, we can really start our lives together. Nothing else matters."

11

The following Sunday, Miriam attended church with Mark. He deferred to her judgment as to when she would be ready to tell people about the baby and explain the situation. She knew it was a time-sensitive issue and she didn't want people to start speculating when her stomach grew to a point where it couldn't be hidden any longer. The reason she held back, however, was because she worried about Mark's family. She was fairly certain Becca and Julia, along with their husbands, would welcome the baby after they got used to the idea. Aunt Claire would be kind about the situation, no matter how she felt. It was Mark's uncle she feared would blow up over the matter. He would want Mark's first child to be a blood-born Bennett, not the offspring of another man. If he couldn't accept Mark's choice to raise the baby as his own, would he try to force Mark to end their marriage? Would he make Mark's work at the mine difficult since he owned the other half?

"What are you thinking about?" Becca probed from beside her on the family pew. "You've been quiet all morning."

"I'm just thinking about my future with Mark."

"And children? I haven't wanted to say anything, but my servants came with me from my brother's house, and they often talk to yours. I don't think they meant to let anything slip on purpose, but there was mention of you being with child."

Miriam sucked in her breath and held it. Did she suspect something about the paternity of the baby? If Becca was good at arithmetic, she'd know soon enough that the baby couldn't possibly be her brother's child.

"You aren't going to tell anyone, are you?"

"My dear sister, you won't be able to keep this baby a secret for much longer—and besides, a baby is a cause to celebrate, not something you should have to hide."

"It is when you're in my situation," Miriam

grumbled under her breath. "No one is going to understand."

"I suppose you mean because the baby belongs to your deceased husband," Becca confirmed that she knew the truth. "If Mark is willing to accept the baby, nothing else matters. You two get to decide how you want to make a home and who the family consists of. It isn't anyone else's business. For the record though, I plan to treat this baby just as I would any other nieces or nephews you should provide me with down the road. There should be enough room in all our hearts to love them all equally."

Becca's response to the baby filled Miriam's heart with warmth. Perhaps she had misjudged Mark's family, and they would take to the news better than she anticipated.

"If I can, let me make one suggestion. Tell the rest of the family before they find out some other way. They'll need time to adjust to the news."

There it was. Becca knew as well as she did that the rest of the family wasn't going to be as receptive as Becca was. Miriam wasn't surprised since her own family was obsessed with carrying on the family name and marrying into the right families.

How could she expect anything different from her husband's family?

"Perhaps we should tell them today at lunch," Miriam suggested. "Everyone will be together and hopefully in a more receptive mood after a good meal."

"I think that's a great idea," Becca confirmed. "And I'll be there, right by your side when you do it. You're not alone in this, Miriam."

"Not alone in what?" Julia inquired as she came up and took a seat next her cousin.

"You'll find out at lunch," Becca said with a smile. "There's no time to talk about it now; service is about to start."

Over the next hour, Pastor Murphy spoke about how God can help sustain someone through trials and tribulations. She wasn't used to the lack of formalness of the service, but found she liked it. Her church back in Russia had a very strict structure that didn't allow for freedom of the Spirit as the Western church did. The pastor's message resonated in her heart, especially his parting words. "If you lean into your faith and trust God, He will carry you through the most difficult of situations." It was exactly what Miriam needed to hear. She just needed to trust that God would help her, and everything would turn out the way it was supposed to.

While the family walked over to the Copper Café, Miriam leaned over and told Mark about her plans to tell the family. "Would you be willing to make the announcement, since it would be better coming from you?"

"I think you're right," he agreed, patting her hand where it rested on his arm. "You seem nervous."

"I am. Their reaction could change everything."

"No, it can't," he stated firmly. "Whatever they say or do, we're in this together now. Nothing will change that."

"That's kind of you to say, but I can't get this uneasy feeling to leave the pit of my stomach."

"Perhaps I can help with that. I have a dreadful joke I've been meaning to tell you."

"Please, anything to take my mind off what you're about to announce."

"When a customer received his meal at a restaurant, he realized something was out of place. He told the waiter, 'See here, I've found a button in my salad.' The waiter replied, "That's all right, sir, it's part of the dressing.""

Miriam couldn't help herself, she let out a sharp

laugh, causing the rest of the family to glance her way for a moment. She covered her mouth as she shook her head, causing her dark curls to bounce around her face. "You're right, that might be the most dreadful joke I've ever heard."

Jim Pierce, the café owner, was standing at the front entrance of the café with his wife, Kate, ready to greet them. "Marriage looks good on you," Jim stated with a wide grin. "It's obvious you made the right decision by marrying this one," he added as he gestured with his head towards Miriam. "Why don't all of you follow me over to one of our larger tables in the back."

Once they were settled in around the table, they placed their orders. Kate scurried off to put them in with the cook, leaving them alone.

"Since we're all together, I want to make an announcement. Miriam and I are going to have a baby."

Everyone's eyes grew round with surprise, and Aunt Claire was the first to speak up. "Wait, I'm confused. How could you possibly know that this soon? You haven't been married long enough for it to make sense."

"We know because Miriam was pregnant when she arrived in Little Ridge."

"And you chose to marry her, anyway?" Mark's uncle growled out in anger. "How foolish could you be to tie yourself to a woman that's carrying another man's child?"

Miriam felt her stomach clench in dread. What was he going to think when he found out that she kept the baby a secret when she arrived in Arizona?

"Uncle Martin, I understand that you're shocked and upset, but how and why I decided to marry Miriam is between myself and my wife. I've made the decision to raise the child as my own, and nothing you're going to say will convince me otherwise."

Miriam's eyes darted to her husband, and instinctively, she reached under the table and squeezed his hand with her own. He was going to protect her and keep the information about when he found out to himself.

"I, for one, think it's wonderful. Babies are a blessing," Becca interjected, reaching out and patting Miriam's arm. "I can't wait to have a little niece or nephew to spoil."

"Me, too," Julia chimed in with a smile. "I love babies and hope to have one of my own soon. It will be wonderful to have a built-in playmate, in the form of a cousin, ready for our own baby."

"Congratulations," Ed said with a nod. "This is wonderful news."

"The baby is lucky; both of you will make great parents," Garrett added.

"Will wonders never cease—a new baby," Aunt Claire stated in a way that made it clear she was still trying to process the news, but she didn't seem upset by it as much as surprised.

"Thank you. We appreciate all of your support," Mark stated, squeezing Miriam's hand in return under the table. "As for you, Uncle Martin, I hope that given some time, you'll come to understand my decision."

They finished up their meal and Mark took Miriam home. "I have a few things I need to do in my study, then I have a surprise for you."

"You do? What is it?"

"If I told you what it was, it would ruin the surprise," he teased.

"Are we going somewhere? At least tell me what I should wear," she pressed. "I don't want to end up at the opera wearing a cotton skirt and blouse."

"Do you even own a cotton anything?"

She shook her head. "You have a point, but still, I want to be properly dressed for the occasion."

"Wear something comfortable. It's just going to be the two of us."

Miriam spent the next half hour getting ready. She picked out a simple satin pink day-dress, hoping that it would work for where he was taking her. She made her way downstairs and entered his study. "I'm all set to go," she declared. "I hope what I'm wearing will work."

Mark glanced up and gave an approving grin. "Indeed it does. You look fetching in that dress."

"Glad you approve," she teased as he came over and took her by the arm.

Tandy met them by the front door with a wicker picnic basket and blanket in her hands. "Here you go, Mr. Bennett. I packed the meal according to your wishes."

"Thank you, Tandy." Mark took the basket and blanket from the servant. "We'll be back in a couple of hours; make sure to have Mrs. Bennett's bath drawn for her when we return."

"We're going on a picnic?" Miriam inquired with surprise as she picked up her sun-hat from the coat rack and placed it on her head.

"I hope you aren't disappointed. Growing up, it was one of my favorite things to do."

"I've never had the pleasure," Miriam admitted. "But I've always thought it sounded so romantic."

"Sometimes your cryptic comments about your past make me wonder about your life in Russia. Maybe during our picnic, you can tell me a little bit about it."

"I thought we agreed to leave my past in the past," she pointed out, hoping he would take the hint and let it go.

"I suppose you're right. I doubt you want to hear about every exploit from my past."

"*Exploit?*" she questioned with raised eyebrows. "Are you trying to bait me into wanting to talk about our pasts?"

"Is it working?"

"Almost," she giggled, playfully smacking the side of his arm. "But you're not going to trick me that easily."

They exited the house and walked the short distance to the riverfront. Mark spread out the blanket and they both took spots on opposite sides of it. He opened the basket that sat between them, and pulled out the cloth-wrapped sandwiches, a container of fresh fruit, macarons, and tin cups for the lemonade.

"Everything looks delicious," she praised, taking

one of the grapes and popping it into her mouth. "You brought all my favorites."

"Of course, I did. This surprise was for you since you've been spending so much time planning the town social with the women's auxiliary."

Little did he know; Miriam was actually working on a completely different project. One that he would find out about soon enough when the time was right.

As they ate their meal, Miriam's attention drifted around the area from one family to the next, each enjoying the late afternoon summer sun just as they were. Several small children were running around the grass, making her wonder if in a few years that might be Mark and her with their own family.

"I can see why you love this place," Miriam mused. "Little Ridge is charming and quaint; it's the perfect place to raise a family."

"Do you want a lot of children?" Mark probed, glancing from her belly back up to her eyes.

"As many as the Lord is willing to bless me with. I love children, and since I was an only child, I've always wanted a large family."

"I'm glad to hear that. I've always imagined if I

met the right woman, I would want at least four children with her."

"Have you met the right woman?" she probed in return.

"I have indeed. I can't imagine ever being with anyone but you, Miriam."

"I feel the same way about you, Mark. It's why I was so scared to tell you about the baby. I thought my secret would ruin everything between us."

"Nothing could do that; I'm yours—heart, mind, and body—if you will have me." He leaned across the blanket and let his lips touch hers. It was a gentle kiss, filled with kindness and love, which had never been a part of her relationship with her first husband. Mark's sweet kiss was exactly what Miriam needed from him, and she kissed him back, hoping that he understood that she wanted every part of him, from this moment forward.

The baby kicked in response, causing Miriam to pull back out of reflex. Without thinking, she reached out and grabbed Mark's hand, then placed it on her belly. "Do you feel that?"

Mark's eyes grew wide as the baby kicked a second time. "I do. It's even stronger than the first time I felt the little one," he said with enthusiasm.

She nodded. "The baby's been doing somersaults for the past week. I've been wanting to share it with you."

"I'm so glad you did," he gushed as he grinned from ear-to-ear. He shifted his hand to the side and pressed lightly. "There, I felt the baby tumble again."

They spent the next half hour talking about the baby and what they needed to do to get ready for the arrival.

"I think I need to stretch," Miriam said, standing up from the blanket. "I can only sit in one spot for so long before my body goes numb from the extra weight. I hope this bulkiness goes away once I have the baby—I'm not used to having such a thick waist."

"Even if it doesn't, you're still the most beautiful woman I've ever seen," he said, standing up beside her and taking her hand in his. "Besides, I like it when a woman has a little meat on her bones."

Miriam liked that he didn't seem to care about the weight she'd gained; the complete opposite of Nicholas, who became angry when she put on a couple of pounds because of the strain of his demanding ways. "It's nice to not have to live in fear that something I do, or don't do, will cause you to become angry with me."

"Did that happen often with your first husband?" Mark probed as he guided her over to the river's edge.

She nodded. "He tried to control everything I did. I didn't have a moment to myself—the palace servants saw to that." Just as the words tumbled from her lips, she wished she could scoop them back up. Her eyes rounded with fear as she covered her mouth with her hand.

"Palace? What palace? Why did you live in a palace?" Mark shouted in confusion.

Miriam could feel the world spinning around her, and she was certain she was going to faint if Mark hadn't reached out to steady her. "I'm not feeling too good. I think I need to sit down again," she whispered, slumping to the ground, not caring that the blanket was several feet away and she was going to land on the mud beside the riverbank.

Mark knelt down beside her. He lifted her chin so that her eyes would meet his own. "I'm sorry I got so excited; you just took me by surprise. You don't have to be afraid of me though. You can tell me anything. Who was your first husband, Miriam?"

"Nicholas Alexander Novikoff, the Grand

Prince of Russia, the one true heir to the Imperial Throne," she recited out of habit.

"Wait, I don't understand. If you were married to a prince, doesn't that make you a princess?"

"It does, but my title doesn't mean anything now that my husband is dead. It's why I had to flee Russia. My husband's brother killed him and I witnessed it. He knew I would tell everyone what I saw, so he blamed me for Nicholas' death. I barely escaped with my life, and I've been in hiding ever since."

Mark wrapped his arm around her shoulders, pulling her close. "That must have been so scary. I can't even imagine what you went through."

"It was one thing when I was only afraid for my own life, but now I have the baby to worry about. If my husband's brother ever finds me, he'll have me killed, and if the emperor finds out about the baby, he'll take the child from me and get rid of me afterwards. I have to stay hidden for both our sakes."

"I promise you, Miriam, I'll keep your secret, and keep you safe. I'll never let anything happen to you."

"I know you want to believe that, but I was chased across the world because the imperial family was determined to make me pay for Nicholas' death. It wasn't until I changed my last name when I arrived in America that I was able to disappear and hopefully escape their reach forever. One slip up, one stupid mistake, however, could mean the end for me and my baby. I have to keep my past a secret for both our sakes."

"Was that why you were so afraid to let Mr. Walker print an article about you in the local newspaper?"

"You know about that?"

He nodded. "Becca told me. She was concerned you were hiding something."

"She wasn't wrong. I've been hiding who I am for so long now, I don't even know who I am anymore."

"I know who you are, Miriam. You're the kind, gentle, compassionate woman I care deeply for. You're a wonderful wife, and you're going to be an even better mother to our children."

"Thank you," she said, choking back her tears. "It's such a relief to not have to keep this from you anymore, and to know you aren't mad at me because I kept it a secret for so long."

"I'm not like your first husband, Miriam. You don't have to ever worry about something you do upsetting me."

"That's good to hear, because you're going to have to put up with me doing this." Miriam swiped away the tears, then removed her boots and stockings. She placed her toes in the water, wiggling them in the cool liquid and enjoying the feel of it sliding between her digits. "I was never allowed to be free back in Russia. Every move I made, every word I said, was critiqued and regulated by the imperial court."

"I don't want to control you or make you feel like you have to hide who you are to make me happy. I love everything about you." Mark reached out and touched the side of her face. "You can be whoever you want to be with me."

Miriam closed the distance between them and placed her lips on his. She hoped it conveyed how much she appreciated his devotion, and how in turn, she loved him just as much.

Mark couldn't believe how much his life had changed in the span of a couple of months. Never would he have thought he'd end up married and a father in the same year.

He put away the last of his papers and checked his watch, insuring that he was on time for dinner with Miriam. She was adamant that he be on time, because Cook was making her favorite dish from Russia.

"Are you sure you don't need me to stay?" Mark asked Garrett as he stood up from his desk. "I don't want to leave you to do all the end of the week paperwork by yourself."

"I'll be fine," Garrett stated as he pointed to the exit. "Go home to your pregnant wife."

"Will do," Mark said, picking up his hat and coat from the rack and putting them on. "Miriam would have my hide if I didn't."

Mark barely made it out the door before two of the workers stopped him to ask questions about the new vein of copper they found. He gave them the quickest answers possible, constantly glancing at his pocket watch to keep track of the time. When he finally left the mine, he pushed his horse to make up the lost minutes.

On his ride home, Mark thought about how happy he was with his life. He never knew what he was missing until he married Miriam. Now, he couldn't imagine his life without her, or the baby in it.

He'd never thought too much about being a father, but now that the time was looming closer and closer, he could feel the excitement rising up in him. The anticipation was building up inside him every day. He could hardly wait until he was finally holding the little bundle in his arms. When he did, Mark knew he would fall instantly in love with the baby, just like he did with Miriam. He realized now that his heart was capable of loving far more than he ever knew possible.

Mark rushed through the door, placing his hat

and coat on the rack. "I know, I know, I was supposed to be home a half hour ago. It couldn't be helped. Two of the miners…" His words trailed off when he turned to find his friends and family standing in the foyer of his home.

"Surprise," they yelled in unison, just as Garrett came in behind him and patted him on the back.

"Tell me, we got you," he teased in a whisper. "Or at least pretend we did so Miriam isn't disappointed. You don't want to make a pregnant woman cry."

"No need to pretend, I had no idea," he stammered out in shock. "Miriam planned all of this?"

"I did, with a little help from your family and friends," Miriam explained as she came over and wrapped her arm through his. "Happy Birthday, Mark."

"You didn't have to do all of this," he said, his cheeks burning from all the attention.

"I know, but I wanted to. You've taken such good care of me since I got here, I wanted to do something for you for a change."

They made their way into the dining room where the table was set up with a massive buffet of food. The guests took plates and piled them with portions of appetizers, meats, and side-dishes.

"I had Cook make all your favorites, and I special-ordered a carrot cake from the bakery in Yuma." A three-tiered cake with buttercream frosting sat at one end of the table, with several unlit candles on the very top layer. "I hope you're happy with everything."

"I've never had anyone make me feel so special," he confessed.

"I'm glad, because you do the same for me."

Mark leaned over and kissed his wife's lips, not caring that they were in a room filled with all of their friends and family. He loved his wife, and he didn't care who knew it.

The next hour was spent enjoying the food as the guests mingled and talked.

"So, Mark, do you like the town social?" Becca teased as she elbowed her brother.

"Do you mean the whole time you were supposed to be planning the social, you were putting this party together for me?" Mark asked in shock.

"Well, the majority of it was for your birthday, but we are going to have a town social at the end of the summer. We also started preparing for the Fourth of July celebration."

"You've really outdone yourselves," Aunt Claire

gushed as she came up to the group. "I can tell you put a lot of thought into what Mark would like."

"It was all Miriam," Becca pointed out. "I just helped her when she asked."

"I can see you really care about my nephew, and you've taken the time to get to know him. Some wives spend their whole lives and never know their husbands well enough to plan a party they'd actually like."

"Thank you. It means a lot to hear you say that."

"My sister's right; you're a good fit for my nephew," Uncle Martin confirmed as he approached them. "It isn't often I have to say this, but I was wrong about you, Miriam. Over the past few weeks, you've proven yourself to be exactly what Mark needs. It's clear you belong together."

"Thank you, Uncle Martin. Your approval is the best birthday present you could give me."

The guests made their way into the backyard, where the garden was dotted with gas lamps and an area was set up for dancing. A band was playing music, encouraging couples to gather in the center.

"Would you like to dance with me?" Mark requested as he held out his hand to his wife.

She placed her hand in his. "I would love to."

He pulled her into the middle of the area and gathered her into his arms. Their bodies melted together, swaying to the music in perfect harmony.

"Doesn't it make you dizzy to waltz?" Miriam inquired as she looked up into his eyes.

"Yes, sometimes," he replied, curious as to where she was going with the odd question.

"Well, you must get used to it. It's the way of the whirled."

His brows came together in a furrow as he tilted his head in confusion. "I'm not sure what you mean by that."

"Don't you get it? It's my birthday present to you—the perfect dreadful joke on your special day. Way of the *whirled*, you know, like when you whirl someone around in a waltz."

Suddenly, the joke clicked into place and made sense, just like their relationship. One moment, he wasn't sure if he made the right decision marrying Miriam, and in the next, he couldn't imagine loving anyone but her. He knew it to be his deepest truth, and he couldn't wait another second before telling her. "I love you, Miriam. I've known it for a while, but I wasn't ready to tell you until right now."

"I love you too, Mark; more than I ever thought I could love anyone."

The evening wrapped up and the guests trickled away, leaving them finally alone close to midnight. Miriam was busy cleaning up the mess, but Mark stopped her. "Let the servants get that. I have something I need to show you."

Mark guided her into his study where he pulled out a piece of paper and handed it over to Miriam. She looked down at it, then back up at her husband, with shock clearly written across her face. "I can't believe you did this. It's more than I could have ever asked for."

"I want you to know, I consider the baby you're carrying to be as much mine as yours. This legal document just declares that truth to the rest of the world so no one can ever dispute it."

"The first-born child of Miriam Bennett, my lawfully wedded wife, is to be treated as my legal and lawful heir, with every benefit and entitlement such designation deserves. He or she will share in the same inheritance as any other issue from our union," Miriam read the words out loud. "This is an irrevocable, legal declaration that cannot be broken for any reason."

Tears filled her eyes as she placed the document down on the desk. She reached out and placed her hand on the side of his cheek. "I never knew one piece of paper could fill my heart with such a deep well of joy. I'm so glad God brought you into my life."

He placed his hand over hers, gripping it tightly as he let his mouth drift down to claim her lips for his own. It was a strong kiss, filled with the passion he could no longer contain. Like a bolt of lightning slamming down between them, it sparked a fire that had been smoldering between them for weeks. Miriam's hands reached up and wrapped around his neck, her fingers tangling in his hair at the top of his collar. She sighed against his mouth, causing him to deepen the kiss. By the time he pulled away, they were both breathless, their hearts beating in unison, branding him Miriam's for all time.

The following week, Miriam arrived for knitting club. She was ready to get a head start on the items the soldiers would need for winter, knowing that time would get away from them if they didn't start on the project early.

Miriam entered the church, but instead of it being set up the regular way for the club, the room was decorated with paper streamers and gingham tablecloths. There was food spread on one of the tables, as well as a punch bowl with glass cups. There was also a large cake on another table with the words "Welcome Baby Bennett" scrolled across the center.

"What's going on? What is all this?" Miriam

inquired in confusion. "I thought we were making scarves and socks for the soldiers."

"Oh, that's been moved to next week," June explained with a mischievous smile. "We decided that we'd much rather have a knitting party for your baby."

"It was my idea," Becca said with a wink. "But Julia did most of the planning. She likes it."

"You didn't have to do all of this," Miriam said with shock.

"We wanted to," Julia insisted as she joined them. "As did the rest of the women in town. It's why they're all here."

Miriam glanced around the room, noting that Kate Pierce, Molly Walker, the pastor's wife, and various other women were indeed present for the shower. The only person she didn't see there was Aunt Claire. Somehow, that one absence diminished the happiness in her heart. It hadn't been lost on her that though they had accepted her as Mark's wife, they never mentioned the baby or the child's role in the family. What was it going to take to make them accept the baby as a Bennett?

Over the next couple of hours, the women finished various clothing items the baby would need, and handed them to Miriam for inspection.

Molly Walker, who was a ferocious knitter, completed about three times as many pieces as the other women, causing her pile of items to nearly topple over from the sheer volume.

"I think you've all given me plenty of clothes for the baby," Miriam said with a warm smile. "Why don't we have some cake now?"

"Do you have room for one more item?" she heard Aunt Claire ask from behind her. "I have a piece I'd like to give you."

Miriam's head swiveled to the side as Aunt Claire came around into her view. She held a small, white box, that she handed over to her.

"Please, open it," Aunt Claire encouraged.

Miriam did as the older woman requested. Inside, there was a delicate white knitted gown. "Did you make this?"

Aunt Claire shook her head. "No, it was Mark's christening gown. I thought you should have it for his baby."

Miriam nearly gasped, surprised by the other woman calling the baby Mark's for the first time. "Thank you. I'll cherish it."

"I hope you will invite me to the christening when you decide to have it."

"Of course; you're family."

"Good, because I'm really looking forward to being a great-aunt."

The rest of the afternoon passed with the women giving her advice, explaining the birthing process, and what she would need to know when the baby was a newborn. By the end of the party, Miriam was exhausted, but in a good way.

"Thank you for a lovely afternoon, but I think I need to head home so I can rest."

"Do you want me to walk with you?" Becca offered.

Miriam shook her head. "I'm fine on my own. It isn't very far."

"We'll bring the baby clothes by tomorrow," June informed her. "I have a few of my daughter's outfits that she's outgrown. I want to include them."

After everyone said their goodbyes, Miriam took off down Main Street. She waved as various townspeople passed by, and crossed the street to avoid the saloon, and the men that often hung around outside. It wasn't until she turned down the side street for her house that she felt a sudden sensation that someone was following her.

Quickly, she spun around to see if someone had followed her from the saloon. Her eyes darted back and forth, scanning the area around her. She didn't see anyone, and decided that she was overreacting because she was tired.

Just as she reached the path that led to her house, she felt the same sensation again, as if someone was watching her. A shiver crawled up her spine. Despite her reservations, she knew she had to look again. Her second attempt didn't bring any new results. The street was empty.

"Stop it, Miriam," she chastised herself. "No one is watching you."

Even though she said the words, she didn't believe them. Part of her worried that her past had finally caught up with her. Had someone from the imperial family tracked her down? Were they going to ambush her when she least expected it? Should she tell Mark what she suspected?

"There you are." The door flew open from the other side to reveal Mark standing across the threshold. "I was starting to worry about you."

"I'm sorry; some of the women from town threw a knitting party for the baby, and it went longer than expected."

"That was nice of them, but I'm sure you're tired. Why don't you rest in the parlor while Cook finishes supper?"

"I think that's a great suggestion."

As Miriam laid down on the couch, she tried to push the uneasy feelings away. She needed to accept that she and the baby were safe, and nothing was going to happen to them now that they were safely hidden away in Little Ridge.

A creaking sound downstairs startled Mark and woke him from his sleep. When he heard it a second time and it sounded like it could possibly be footsteps, he decided he had to check it out. Quietly, he climbed out of bed, making sure not to wake Miriam in the process. Just in case he needed it, he pulled out his gun from the nightstand and headed downstairs.

He made it through about half the rooms before he saw a shadowy figure in the corner of the foyer. He moved across the floor, and was about to go up the stairs when Mark shouted, "Stop right there. Who are you and what are you doing in my house?"

The man moved towards him aggressively, and

for the first time, Mark could make out his features. He was tall with dark hair and a jagged scar across his right cheek. He was wearing a leather duster coat and a wide-rimmed cowboy hat pulled low over his dark eyes.

Mark raised his gun and leveled it at the other man. "I asked you a question, and if you keep coming towards me like that, I'm going to shoot you where you stand."

"My name doesn't matter. What does, is that I know who's sleeping upstairs in your bedroom."

"I don't know what you're talking about," Mark rebuffed quickly, though he couldn't help but feel his blood run cold. As he watched the other man, he knew that this wasn't going to end well. The stranger looked ready to do whatever it took to pry Miriam from her home.

"You can deny it all you want, but I know that the woman upstairs is Miriam Novikoff, a runaway Russian princess. What I'm betting you don't know is that there's a bounty on her head the size of Texas, and I'm here to collect on it."

"You aren't taking my wife anywhere."

"If you try to stop me, I'll kill you," the bounty hunter stated coldly. "I can guarantee you, I'm a much quicker shot than you, and I won't hesitate to end you if you get in my way."

"It would be worth it to keep your hands off my wife," Mark growled out. "You're not leaving here with her."

"We'll see about that. The bounty was enough to make it well worth tracking her down, but now that I know she's carrying a baby that isn't yours, I'm betting she's going to be worth double the reward once they find out she's pregnant with the Russian heir to the Imperial Throne."

"If you don't leave right now, you're going to regret it," Mark shouted. "You might think the Russian imperial family is powerful, but as far as Arizona goes, my family is royalty around here."

A noise from the top of the stairs drew both their attention. Miriam was standing in her robe, staring down at them. "What's going on? Who is that man and what's he doing in our house?"

The bounty hunter charged up the stairs, prompting Mark to fire his gun at the other man. The rounds missed the stranger and the revolver was empty after the fifth shot, making it useless. He shoved it in his pants' pocket as he rushed after the stranger, yelling, "Get to our room and lock the door, Miriam."

Just as he ordered, she turned around and bolted down the hallway, the bounty hunter fast on her pursuit.

Mark knew that he had to get to the other man and stop him before he reached Miriam. When he got to the top of the stairs, the bounty hunter turned and fired his gun. Mark barely jumped out of the way in time, but continued to chase after the other man.

Mark found the bounty hunter trying to knock down the door. With him distracted, Mark took the opportunity to charge at him. He knocked the other man to the ground, causing his gun to go flying across the floor. They wrestled back and forth, exchanging blow-for-blow. Several times, the man tried to reach the gun, but Mark pulled him away from it each time.

The door to the bedroom opened and out of the corner of his eye, Mark saw Miriam come out. What was she thinking? She was much safer inside the bedroom than coming out into the hallway. He wanted to shout at her to get back inside, but he didn't want to draw the bounty hunter's attention to her presence.

"Get your hands off my husband," Mark heard

Miriam scream at the top of her lungs. "I have your gun, and I'm pointing it right at you."

Both men stopped fighting and looked up at her from the ground.

"I'm betting you've never fired a gun in your life. I don't think you'll pull the trigger, Princess," the bounty hunter challenged as he scrambled to his feet and moved towards her.

To everyone's surprise, Miriam did just what she threatened and pulled the trigger. The bullet missed. The shock, however, gave Mark just enough time to act. He pulled the gun from his pocket and slammed it into the back of the bounty hunter's head. The man slumped over on the ground.

There was a flurry of footsteps up the stairs as the servants came tumbling into the hallway.

"What happened? Who is that man on the ground?" Mary asked with concern.

"He's an intruder," Mark stated firmly. "I need you to get the sheriff, Tandy, while Cook and Asher tie up the man."

Mark reached out and pulled Miriam towards him. She was shaking like a leaf and her eyes were bright red from crying. "I was petrified he was going to kill you," Miriam cried out as Mark held her in his arms. "It's why I had to do something. I can't live without you."

"And you're never going to have to. I promised you, I'll always keep you safe."

"You can't keep that promise—not when more men like him are just going to keep coming. If he found me, it's just a matter of time before someone else does."

"Trust me, I'll take care of it. Your first husband's family might be the most powerful family in all of Russia, but the Bennett family is a force to be reckoned with here in the West."

Miriam nodded. "I trust you, Mark, always."

"Good, because no matter what it takes, I'm going to keep you and our child safe. I love you, Miriam, and you're everything to me."

"I love you, too," she whispered back as she leaned up and placed her lips on his.

Despite the salty tears and the sticky sweat, the kiss did its job, comforting them both and letting them know that come what may, they would face it together as husband and wife.

EPILOGUE

6 months later

"I can't believe how Nancy gets more beautiful every time I see her," Becca gushed as she picked up her niece and held the swaddled bundle in her arms.

"She's the most perfect thing I've ever seen," Julia added as she looked over her cousin's shoulder. "When do I get to hold her?"

"I just got her myself," Becca argued with a huff. "Give me a few minutes with her, will you?"

Aunt Claire stood up, walked across the parlor,

and scooped the baby out of Becca's arms. "Great-aunts trump regular aunts every time."

The rest of the group laughed, besides Becca, who stared at her aunt with a miffed look on her face. She crossed her arms and leaned back in the chair. "Somebody around here needs to have another baby so I can hold one."

"Are you offering?" Garrett teased from beside her.

Becca's eyes grew wide for a moment before she shrugged. "I wouldn't object if it happened."

"I'm glad to hear everything is in order with fixing the problem with the Russians," Uncle Martin stated from his seat across the room.

"It helps to have enough money to pay off all the right people," Mark confirmed. "The bounty has been officially rescinded."

The Bennett family attorney arranged for the bounty hunter to be placed in a remote prison where he could never tell anyone that mattered about the Russian princess he nearly captured in Arizona. Once he was taken care of, Mark had a fleet of private investigators spread a rumor that a Russian woman fitting Miriam's description was killed in a drowning accident in Oregon. Mark had one of the private investigators track down a piece of the imperial jewelry and place it with a body to verify the identity. After a couple of months waiting, it was confirmed that word got back to Russia, and the imperial family officially called off the search for the princess. Miriam and the baby were finally, officially safe.

"I'm just glad it's all over. I thought I would have my past hanging over me for the rest of my life. It feels good to know I don't have to worry about that anymore."

"I'm still just trying to wrap my mind around the fact that we have a princess in the family now," Becca teased. "To think, Uncle Martin, all this time, you thought she didn't come from good enough stock to marry Mark. In actuality, it turns out, our stock wasn't good enough for her."

"Listen here, Becca Bennett Casner, we may not be imperialists, but we are Arizona royalty. Never forget where you come from, niece."

"I can't agree more. I'm proud to be a Bennett," Miriam said with a big smile. "And I'm going to raise my daughter to be proud to be one, too."

"So you mean we don't have to call you, your Imperial Highness, then?" Mark teased.

"Only you do, when we're alone," she jested back.

"That reminds me, I have another dreadful joke for you," Mark announced.

"Oh, no, not again," Garrett whined. "I'm so sick of hearing them."

"This is my house, and I want to hear his joke," Miriam demanded with a wink. "You can plug your ears if you don't want to listen."

"Which is the favorite word with women?" Mark asked as he looked around the room.

Everyone shook their heads, making it clear they didn't have the answer.

"The last one," Mark answered, causing the entire group to laugh at the dreadful joke that had a bit of truth behind it.

"Promise me you'll never stop doing that," Miriam said as she leaned into her husband's frame on the couch.

"Doing what?"

"Making me laugh."

"How could I? It was part of our agreement in the advert. We always have to laugh at each other's dreadful jokes."

The Bennett family spent the rest of the evening discussing the mine, the church service on Sunday, and the details for Nancy's christening.

"I hate to give her up, but it's getting rather

late," Julia said as she placed Nancy in her mother's arms. "I'll come by later this week to spend some more time with the both of you."

"I'll look forward to it."

Mark shut the door on the last family member to leave, then turned to face his wife. "I love having them over, but they sure do wear me out."

"But it's worth it. I always wanted a big, close family, and you've given that to me. Truthfully, you've given me so many blessings, I can't keep track of them all."

"It goes both ways, you know. Every day you give me something wonderful." Mark leaned over and kissed his wife on the lips, then his daughter on the forehead. "I'm going to go get ready for bed. Come join me when you're done down here."

Miriam stared down at her sleeping infant daughter and knew that everything was right in the world. It didn't matter what they escaped from, or how they ended up where they were. All that mattered was that they were right where they were supposed to be, living their life with the man who chose to love them both for the rest of their lives. Miriam couldn't ask for anything more.

Early Spring of 1881
Lake Hope, Pennsylvania

The baby's earsplitting cries echoed down the hall, causing Miranda Barton to cover her head with a pillow. Nearly every night for the past six months, her niece, Eleanor, woke bellowing at one in the morning. Her precise timing would be commendable if it wasn't so exasperating.

"Please, Elle, just for one night, stop crying," Miranda mumbled into the mattress of her bed. "I just need one good night's sleep before I head to Texas in two days."

As if to show who was in charge of the house, Eleanor's cries increased both in tempo and shrillness.

Miranda threw the pillow off her head and rolled over, swinging her legs over the side of the bed. She might as well check on her sister, Elizabeth, who would no doubt be tending the baby while her husband, Albert, was fast asleep. It always stunned her how that man could sleep so soundly through such a grating nightly occurrence.

After slipping on her robe, Miranda padded down the hallway until she reached the nursery. She pushed the door open and observed from the threshold. Elizabeth was in the rocking chair, gently moving it back and forth in an effort to soothe the baby. Eleanor wasn't having any of it though. Her tiny pink face scrunched up in a wretched scowl before another bloodcurdling scream projected from her mouth.

"Did you try offering her some bread with a little brandy on it?" Miranda inquired, moving further into the room. "Jane said it could help."

"Yes, I tried it, and Elle promptly spit it out. She only cried harder afterward, making it that much more difficult to calm her down. Jane might be the pastor's wife, but she isn't an expert on everything, though she seems to think so," Elizabeth stated sarcastically with a shake of her head. "I don't know how much more of this I can take, Miranda. What if Eleanor never outgrows this behavior?"

"Here, give her to me for a bit." Miranda reached out to take her niece. "You look as though you might break down and weep at any moment." Miranda placed Eleanor's stomach against her own chest and gently patted her back as she paced the floor. Within a few minutes, the motion did its trick and her niece drifted off to sleep.

"How did you do that?" Elizabeth marveled, with a hint of envy in her voice. "It never ceases to amaze me how good you are with her. I don't know what I'm going to do without you when you leave in two days."

"It's all in the walk," Miranda said, continuing to pace back and forth to make sure Eleanor didn't wake up. "You just need to keep a steady cadence, and pat her back at the same time."

Elizabeth shook her head. "You make it sound so easy, but I've tried doing exactly that. It's not what you do, or even how you do it. It's you, Miranda; you have a gift when it comes to children. They bond with you in a way that is very special."

Miranda hoped her sister was right. She was going to need that special gift if she was going to be capable of taking on the job of being a mother to twin almost three-year-old boys. When she saw Cade Tanner's advert for a mail order bride in the *Matrimonial Times*, she nearly passed it up when it mentioned the children. She hadn't been sure if she was interested in having an instant family, but when all the other adverts were placed by morally bankrupt scoundrels or old men looking for a young wife, she decided children might be the least of her problems.

Elizabeth insisted that she didn't need to leave, but Miranda didn't want to be a burden anymore. Her sister and her husband were barely surviving on his income as a constable. Miranda supposed she could have tried to get a job herself, but with no education or experience to speak of, reputable jobs for a woman were scarce.

"You'll be fine," Miranda encouraged, as she placed Eleanor in her crib. "You're a great mother. Eleanor will get through this, and soon all her fussiness will be a distant memory."

"I hope you're right, but that doesn't change the fact I'm going to miss you so much when you leave."

"I'll miss you, too, but you can come visit any time."

"I'd like that," Elizabeth stood up and squeezed her sister's hand. "I'll pray for safe travels for you. It's a long train ride to Texas."

TOMORROW, Miranda would be setting off for her new life in Rockwood Springs. All of her belongings were packed and ready for the trip. She had her ticket and traveling money her future husband had wired to her safely tucked in her tapestry bag.

A nervous excitement was in the pit of her stomach as she held Eleanor in her arms. Gently, she patted the infant's back just the way she liked it. Once Elizabeth and Albert returned from the market, they would help her with her final arrangements before departure. In no time at all, she was going to be barreling down the rails heading to Cade and his sons.

"I'm going to miss you, Elle, but this is going to be better for everyone," Miranda whispered in her niece's ear. She didn't like the idea of leaving her behind, but it had to be this way. "I know I'm a burden to your parents, and that isn't fair. I need to find a way to make a life for myself. Cade and his boys need me, and I can make a life with them. I hope one day you'll be able to come and visit me." She turned her face and gently kissed the baby's cheek, trying to repress the tears that were forming in the corners of her eyes.

There was a knock at the door, and Miranda moved from the parlor into the entry hall of the house. Maybe it was some of the women from church coming to say goodbye. Most of them hadn't been the most supportive in the beginning when she told them her plans to be a mail order bride, but there were still a few that might come to wish her farewell.

She opened the door and on the other side stood men wearing dark blue constable uniforms. She recognized both men from her sister's wedding as well as from church. What put her on edge was they both had a look in their eyes that didn't bode well for why they were there.

"Good morning, Miss Barton, can we come in?" the taller of the men asked politely.

She nodded, stepping back to let them enter. "Please, follow me into the parlor."

"Miss Barton, you might want to sit down for what we need to tell you," the shorter, portly man said with a sad smile. "This is going to be difficult to hear."

Miranda's stomach tightened with dread. "What is it?"

"There was a robbery at the market today. The owner of one of the stores pulled a gun to defend himself, but the thieves shot back. Unfortunately, your sister and Albert were caught in the crossfire."

"Are they going to be all right? Are they at the hospital?" Miranda inquired, already figuring out in her head who she would ask to watch Eleanor while she went to tend to her family. She'd have to write her future husband, of course, and explain she would be delayed for a few days, possibly weeks, but hopefully he would understand.

"I'm sorry to say, Miss Barton, neither of them survived. Their wounds were too severe," the taller constable informed her with a sympathetic look.

Miranda's whole body started to shake, her knees were suddenly weak, and the room was spinning out of control.

"Miss Barton, here, let me help you. You don't want to drop the baby," the shorter constable shouted as he came up beside her and guided her onto the sofa nearby.

The baby, what was going to happen to

Eleanor? She was an orphan now, just like Miranda. She never hoped to share such a heartbreaking connection with her niece.

"Can we get someone for you, Miss Barton? Do you have any family nearby?" the shorter constable offered.

She shook her head, tears falling down her cheeks in rapid succession. "My sister was all the family I had left, she and my niece. What is to become of the baby?"

"Albert didn't have any family left either, did he?" the taller constable asked.

She shook her head, and forced herself to swallow the lump in her throat so she could answer. "We were all orphans. We often lamented that it was what bound us all together."

"I suppose you would be charged with taking care of her then, if you're willing," the taller man explained. "You're the only family she has left."

Miranda looked down at her sleeping niece. Eleanor was her responsibility now. She needed to do whatever it would take to take care of her. Her protective instincts kicked in. She wasn't sure what she was going to do, but she needed help.

"Can you fetch Pastor Phillips and his wife for me?" she inquired.

The taller constable nodded, then leaned over and whispered to the other man, who a couple of moments later, scurried off towards the front door.

"I can stay with you until they arrive if you'd like," he offered.

She nodded, the constable accepting the gesture as a sign that he could take a seat in the nearby chair.

They sat in silence while they waited, neither of them having any words that could make the situation more palatable. Eleanor started to stir, causing Miranda to shift in her seat. She hoped the baby couldn't sense the tension in her body. The last thing she needed was for her niece to wake up and start crying.

A half hour later, the constable returned with the middle-aged pastor and his wife. It was clear from the expressions on their faces that the constable already told them what had happened.

"Oh my, dear, I'm so sorry," Jane stated in a soothing tone as she took a seat next to Miranda on the couch. "We're here for you, whatever you need."

"Thank you," she pushed out through the lump in her throat, trying to respond the way she was raised to do.

"Do you want us to take a letter to the post office to be sent to that man you were planning to marry in Texas? I'm assuming that absurd idea isn't happening now," Jane stated in a way that made it clear she didn't approve.

Miranda hadn't thought about Cade since she found out about her sister and Albert's deaths. It didn't mean that she didn't want to follow through with her commitment, because she did. She just wasn't sure how she could do that now that she had Eleanor to consider.

"Jane, I can handle that on my own. What I need help with is planning the funeral. I don't know the first thing about it since Elizabeth took care of it for our parents."

"I can handle all of that in the next couple of days," Pastor Phillips offered.

"No, tonight," Miranda stated firmly. "I can use the little bit of money my sister had saved up for the funeral but it has to be done tonight."

"Why is that, dear?" Jane asked with confusion. "That's awfully quick."

"Because, I have a train ticket I need to use tomorrow. I need all of this settled before I go."

Jane's eyes grew round with shock. "You're not seriously thinking of still going to Texas, are you?"

"I don't have much choice, Jane. I know my sister and Albert were already in a dire financial situation. It's why I was leaving in the first place, so I wouldn't be a burden on them anymore. The funeral will take up what little savings they had, so afterward, I have to go to Texas and marry Cade Tanner."

If Miranda had the money, she would've sent a telegram to Cade and told him about her new unexpected circumstances. She didn't have enough money, however, to both bury Elizabeth and Albert and send a telegram, nor the time to send a letter and wait for his reply. She also couldn't find it in herself to beg others to help take care of her and Eleanor. Everyone was having a difficult time providing for their own families since the mill burned down six months prior. It was the major source of income for the town.

"At the very least, then, you should leave Eleanor with us," Jane suggested. "Such a long trip across the country would be difficult on a baby. Besides, you have no idea what's waiting for you at the end of it. Would your intended even want another, unexpected mouth to feed?"

Miranda worried about that, too. Would Cade be upset if she arrived with a baby in her arms?

He'd placed an advert for a mail order bride, not a mail order baby. Would he turn them both out once she got there?

Her mind flashed to the last letter she received from him.

I WILL NOT LIE to you, Miranda. My heart still aches for my dearly departed wife. It is wounded and needs time to heal. I know; however, my children do not have the luxury of waiting while that happens. They need a mother now.

I love children, and know that I have the capacity to love as many as the Lord is willing to bless us with through our marriage. I vow to you I will be a kind and considerate husband, just as I am a father.

SHE HAD to believe from the promises he made in his letter, that if she brought Eleanor with her, he would take her in as his own.

Dakota Territory, 1885

The sprawling Great Plains of North America continued to pass by through the window of the train. The steep, flat-topped hills, better known as buttes, dominated the landscape of the James River Valley. Soon Cara McGregor would be arriving in the town of Mitchell, where her whole life would change forever.

She read the letter from her future husband another time, still trying to accept that she was traveling out West to meet the man willing to marry her. James Cassidy sounded like a good man, a man she could find contentment with, since love wasn't in the cards for her.

Considering her reputation back in her hometown of Hull, Massachusetts, she was glad the man hadn't requested to know more about her family situation. It wasn't good. She left behind a place filled with Irish folk from the Old Country, whom by the end of her time in Hull, treated her like a leper because of what happened with her parents.

She wished she could have gone back to that day and been at the house when her mother was killed. If she had seen what happened instead of being off with her beau, the townspeople wouldn't have blamed her father and hung him two months later for the crime.

She not only lost her parents that day, but her beau along with any future prospects of marriage, since everyone in town viewed her as the spawn of the devil himself. It was as if everyone forgot what a good man her father had been; looking out for his neighbors, helping at the church, and taking care of his family.

The little money her parents had saved ran out by the end of the second month. She couldn't get a job for the same reasons as she couldn't land a husband. All that was left was to start over somewhere else, and she remembered that Josephine Little had found a groom out West through a mail-order advertisement. With nothing left to lose, Cara found herself scouring The Matrimonial Times.

She could still remember the words of Mr. Cassidy's advert in the newspaper. *Needed, Wife. South Dakota widower seeks a kind, faithful woman to run his household on his farm, to support his work, and rear his three children. Due to conditions in the rural area, only a strong, diligent woman of fortitude and grit need reply.*

Cara should have dismissed it out of hand, considering she had no business doing any of the work he required, but something about the unspoken plea in the request pulled at Cara's heart. She needed a new life, and she could help this man while gaining one. What could it hurt to answer?

Two letters and a month later, she was headed out West with only two bags, and her gumption to make the marriage work. She hoped she was able to live up to her new family's expectations, though she had little experience in running a household or mothering children. Her best example was her own mother, who had been loving, helpful, and always there for her. She hoped to provide the same care for her new wards. She was resolved to be the best match for Mr. Cassidy, rather than just a misfit for his family.

Deciding she could use some air, Cara stood

from her seat in the car she shared with a family and a widow traveling to Oregon. She slipped the letter into her pocket, and made her way towards the back of the train. She was about to exit through the back door, when a man came up and blocked her path.

"Why aren't you the prettiest little thing I've ever seen?" the man said with a wag of his eyebrows. He reached out and grabbed a strand of her hair, rubbing it between his fingers and thumb. "I've always had an inkling for redheads."

She shrank back, not liking how close the man was, or the fact he felt justified enough to touch her. "I'll just be going now," she said, trying to push past him to return from the way she came.

Putting out his arm to block her path, he observed, "I thought you were headed to the back of the train? No one's around by the way, so we have the whole section to ourselves."

"I've changed my mind," Cara declared, raising her chin in defiance, while trying to muster her bravest face.

"You needn't hurry off on my account," the man said, leaning in towards her until she could smell the repugnant odor of liquor on his breath. "I've got all the time in the world."

"Well, I don't," she stated tartly. "I have people waiting for me back in my car."

"I don't think so, missy. I've been watching you for a while, and you're traveling alone. Ain't no one worrying about your whereabouts. I doubt anyone would care what happens to you," he snarled, pushing his body against hers as his hand started to roam all over her body.

"Don't touch me," she screamed, squirming against him in anger. "Get your hands off me."

"Did I tell you, that's my favorite part about redheads? Nothin' more appealin' than a redhead's temper. I love it when they get all feisty," he said with a leering grin of pleasure.

Cara froze, realizing that this man wanted her to fight him. It made him excited, and that was the last thing she wanted to encourage.

As she stood perfectly still, she slowly moved her hand down her side. She finally reached the strap inside the hidden insert of her pocket where she carried a small knife. She whipped it out as fast she could, pushing it towards the man's chest.

"If you don't get away from me right now, I'm going to make you a new hole."

The man's eyes grew wide in shock for a few moments before he narrowed them in anger. "Are you sure you can use that knife, missy? I'm bettin' you've never stabbed a man. It's messy, with a lot of blood." He reached out and tried to grab the knife from her, but she dodged his reach.

"It's better than the alternative," she shouted. "I won't have you ruin me."

"Can't ruin something that's already tarnished," he barked out. "You wouldn't be traveling all alone if you were a good woman."

The man lunged at her again. This time his hand made contact with hers, causing them to wrestle for control of the knife. She was about to lose her grip on the hilt when a group of miners entered the car.

"What's going on here?" one of the men shouted with a look of shock on his face.

Her attacker looked fearful for the briefest of moments before he accused, "This thief tried to rob me. I was coming out back to get some air, when she tried to pickpocket me. When I confronted her, she pulled a knife on me."

"That's not what happened," Cara protested. "I was the one coming out back to get air when he accosted me. He had vile intentions, so I had to pull my knife to protect myself."

"What respectable woman would need to carry

a knife around?" the attacker countered. "Only someone who has a devious nature."

"I'm traveling alone, so I brought one of my father's knives along for protection," Cara said, trying to explain away how bad the situation looked on her part.

She could tell from the miners' looks, they doubted her story, and her explanation sounded ridiculous even to her own ears.

"Perhaps one of us should go get the conductor to sort this matter out," a second man suggested.

"I think that's a good idea. I would like to tell him all about how this thief behaved," her attacker stated with confidence. "She'll hang for trying to kill me. I'll make sure of it."

A shiver crawled up Cara's back as she realized this man wanted to make her pay for not getting his way with her. If she didn't escape right now, she was going to end up dangling from a hangman's noose. Glancing out the window, she realized they were slowing down as they approached a set of curves on the rail line. If she jumped off the train now, she'd only suffer a few bumps and bruises, a much better alternative.

Without another thought, Cara turned and rushed towards the door. She swung it open, and flung herself through it. For just a split second, she paused as she came to the edge of the iron railing. Knowing she had no choice, she climbed over and threw herself from the side.

The left side of her body met the ground with a hard thud, right before she started rolling down the small hill. She could feel the dirt and rocks tearing at her flesh; however, she made herself ignore the pain and focus on getting as far away from the train as possible. If she got arrested, it would end badly for her. No one at home would vouch for her, considering her family's history, and some would even say that it made sense that she turned out just like her father. She would be assumed guilty simply because of her family's past.

The shouts of the men from the train echoed around Cara as she rushed along the bank of the James River. Slowly, they faded as she slipped away into her surroundings, praying she would find some way to survive out in the frontier wilderness.

Late Spring of 1877
Outskirts of Abilene, Texas

The sun was stretched low across the late-day sky as Deputy Sheriff Jake Bolton pushed his horse through the prairie flats. A herd of Texas longhorns grazed on the thick fields of golden grass along the road as Jake galloped past the livestock.

He heard the screeching sound of a bird above, causing him to raise his hand over his brow to scan the horizon for the creature. Just as he located the white-tailed hawk, it swooped down and snatched up a small creature from the ground. Such was the cycle of life in the rural Texas countryside.

In his head, Jake went over the details of the investigation he was working on which brought him to the outlying small towns that dotted the northeast corner of Taylor County. The third general store in two weeks had been robbed by the infamous Grimes Brothers.

Jake was tasked with following up the newest lead after a local stagecoach company out of Woody, Texas telegraphed the sheriff's office. One of the drivers had seen two men fitting their descriptions on the road between Woody and Rockwood Springs. The brothers were armed and dangerous, and Jake wanted nothing more than to free the county of their threat.

In the distance, clouds were rolling into sight and the smell of rain was in the air. It wasn't surprising since sporadic showers were common during this time of year. He needed to get to Woody before the sun set and he got caught in the downpour.

EXHAUSTED from a long day of work, Rebecca Caldwell used the sleeve of her blue calico dress to wipe the sweat from her brow; grateful to be finishing up the last of the outside chores. She still needed to prepare dinner for the family, but at least she would be inside before the rain started.

After pulling the last shirt from the clothesline, she pushed several blonde curls out of her face which had come loose from her bun while she worked.

Rebecca made her way around the side of the farmhouse which sat on the same property as the family business—the local livery. As she entered the barn-like structure, she looked around and located her father in front of one of the stalls.

"Father, I'm done working outside and wanted to let you know dinner will be ready in about an hour."

Although brilliant with a horse, Mr. Caldwell often got lost in his thoughts while working with them. He needed constant reminding to finish up his work on time as he often forgot to come in for meals.

The middle-aged, thin man with peppered brown hair and blue eyes— the same color as Rebecca's—glanced up from combing down the colt he had been training all day. "Thank you for reminding me. I'll make sure to not forget this time."

With a nod of her head, Rebecca turned around and moved towards the house. She saw her younger sister, Lydia, run past, and a few moments later, her younger brother, Georgie, chase after, calling, "You better find a good hiding place; I'm gonna find you."

Rebecca smiled to herself at the cuteness of her siblings. Lydia was like a miniature version of Rebecca with her curly blonde hair and blue eyes. Being only ten, she still loved dolls and playing games with the local children. Georgie was sandwiched between them at the age of fourteen and was a rascal at heart. He was getting to the age where he was playing less and noticing girls more, but every once in a while, Lydia could still talk him into playing with her.

As she heard Georgie stomping around the yard looking for Lydia, she reminisced on a time—years ago—when she was able to be carefree like that. She had been forced to grow up quickly when her mother's condition worsened. Rebecca had to take over running the family home and caring for her siblings. She justified her lost childhood as preparation for married life; it would make her a better candidate for a wife.

Although not of spinster age at twenty-one,

Rebecca knew it was time for her to start considering finding a husband. Life was hard on the Texas prairie and she needed a man to protect her when her father was no longer able to do so. She wanted to marry for love, but the practicality of finding it was not wasted on her. She knew there was a real possibility she might have to settle for a relationship built solitarily on friendship.

As Rebecca climbed the back steps of the house, she heard her brother and sister laugh with merriment. Apparently, Georgie had found Lydia after all. Rebecca made her way into the kitchen where she pulled out several pots and pans to start the evening meal.

THE WIND HOWLED in Jake's ear as it raced along the back of his neck, sending a shiver up his spine. He had hoped to make it to Woody before the onslaught, but the clouds had other ideas. Jake pulled the rim of his hat down to shield his eyes from the frigid rain pelting his body.

Jake tightened his grip on the reins to his brown and white paint horse, Ginger, as he pulled her to a stop. Up ahead, the rain had washed out part of the road.

With a heavy sigh, he debated what to do. If he backtracked in order to find a route that bypassed that section of the road, it would delay his arrival in Woody by at least a half day. Should he brave it by trying to cross the muddy area?

Deciding it would be better to take his chances, Jake prodded Ginger forward, gently pushing his spurs into the horse's side. Usually an obedient horse, it surprised Jake when she sidestepped and hesitated. Did his horse sense something Jake couldn't see?

With a scan of the area, Jake resolved going ahead was still the best option. Jumping down from his horse, he guided Ginger through the murky water. Coaxing her, he said, "Come on, girl, just a little further. I promise you some primo hay and maybe even a sugar cube or two if you get us safely to Woody by nightfall."

Reluctantly, the horse complied and started to walk along the road behind Jake. The further they traveled, the deeper the mud got until both of them were finding it difficult to move.

Just as Jake worried they would become stuck, a lightning bolt came crashing down right in front of them. Neighing in fear, Ginger reared up causing Jake to be knocked down. With a hard thud, he pummeled to the ground, knocking the air from his lungs.

The mud sloshed around him, pulling his body deep into its thick grasp. Jake blinked once, twice, three times before he tried to sit up from the murky ground. A sharp pain radiated up his abdomen. Recognizing the feeling, he knew the fall had earned him a set of bruised ribs.

With concerted effort, Jake climbed to his feet. As he turned to find Ginger, his eyes grew round with concern. The horse was whimpering and she wasn't placing weight on her right leg. Jake moved towards her and gently lifted the leg from the muddy water. There was a huge crack on her hoof as well as a deep gash at the first joint. What could have caused such a horrific injury?

He placed his hand into the mud. Below the surface, he felt the edge of something rough and hard. Although he couldn't see it, he was certain it was a large rock, most likely brought down by a mudslide from a nearby hill.

Jake reached out and took Ginger's muzzle into his hands. He leaned his face against hers and whispered, "It's all right, girl. You did the best you could. This is my fault. I shouldn't have pushed you so hard."

With deep regret, Jake contemplated what to do. When a horse broke its leg, there was only one thing to do, but he hoped it wasn't the case.

He tried to swallow the lump of pain in his throat. Ginger was the last connection to his past; a gift from his wife, Marjorie, during their final Christmas together. She had saved up money to purchase the horse for two years, washing laundry at the Abilene Inn.

Lightning cracked across the sky, illuminating the air for just a moment. Not far off in the distance, Jake saw the flickering gas lights of a small town. Maybe Ginger could make it to Rockwood Springs—which was closer than Woody—if he helped her stay off the leg.

As he ran his hand through his hair, he sighed. With a heavy heart, he removed the saddle and attached bag from Ginger to make her load lighter. With determined resolve, he started the walk to Rockwood Springs with Ginger beside him.

Grab your copy of Lawfully Loved.

I hope you have enjoyed Mail Order Miriam, and plan to read my first book, Mail Order Miranda, in the Widows, Brides, and Secret Babies series. You can also continue to read my other historical series such as Mail Order Mix-up which starts with *Mail Order Misfit*. Also, if you would like to find out how Rebecca and Jake, Abigail and Levi, Naomi and Emmett, and Judy and Paul, all end up together, check out my lawkeeper series. You can grab all of them in my Historical Lawkeeper box set which gives you the entire collection at a significantly reduced price or grab any of them off my Amazon author page.

Your opinion and support matters, so I would greatly appreciate you taking the time to leave a review. Without dedicated readers, a storyteller is lost. Thank you for investing in my stories. If you would like more info, please join my newsletter and

get a free novella and short story just for signing up
for my <u>Newsletter</u>.

Jenna Brandt

Most Books are Free in Kindle Unlimited too!

Widows, Brides, and Secret Babies-mail order bride stories with a twist. What happens when a bride arrives pregnant or with a secret child? Find out in this all new series.

Mail Order Miranda

Mail Order Miriam

Mail Order Mixup Series-mail order bride books about women venturing out West to make new lives for themselves. What happens when they decide to take a chance on love along the way?

Mail Order Misfit

Mail Order Misstep (coming soon)

Mail Order Miscast (coming soon)

The Civil War Brides Trilogy-during the bloodiest conflict on American soil, two families struggle in the South to not only survive but to thrive.

<u>Saved by Faith</u>

<u>Freed by Hope</u>

<u>Healed by Grace</u>

Border Brides Series-centered around the Old West border towns and the brides who end up there looking for a new start.

Discreetly Matched

<u>June's Remedy</u>

<u>Becca's Lost Love</u>

Pinkerton Matchmaker Series-as female agents were few and far between, Mr. Gordon came up with the idea of expanding the detective agency by pairing qualified women with a male agent for training, guidance and undercover work. These women came from all demographics – some were looking for a new life, some seeking challenge, some wanting to pave the way for future generations of women. The only caveat – the women wouldn't be a member of the Agency until their first assignment had been completed.

<u>An Agent for Nadine</u>

<u>An Agent for Gwendolyn</u>

Silverpines Series-centered around the fictional town

of Silverpines, Oregon, during the turn of the 20th century. When a disaster takes most of the men, the women are left to save the town by placing mail-order groom advertisements. Get to know the various lovable characters and their stories from some of todays bestselling historical authors.

<u>Wanted: Tycoon</u>

<u>The Tycoon's Sister</u>

Bride Herder Series-take one failed rancher turned matchmaker and ten unexpected brides at once with no clue as to who wanted them. What could go wrong?

<u>Herd to Please</u>

The Window to the Heart Saga is a recountal of the epic journey of Lady Margaret, a young English noblewoman, who through many trials, obstacles, and tragedies, discovers her own inner strength, the sustaining force of faith in God, and the power of family and friends. In this three-part series, experience new places and cultures as the heroine travels from England to France and completes her adventures in America. The series has compelling themes of love, loss, faith and hope with an exceptionally gratifying conclusion.

Trilogy

<u>The English Proposal</u> (Book 1)

<u>The French Encounter</u> (Book 2)

<u>The American Conquest</u> (Book 3)

Spin-offs

<u>The Oregon Pursuit</u> (Book 1)

<u>The White Wedding</u> (Book 2)

<u>The Christmas Bride</u> (Book 3)

(Free when you join my newsletter)

<u>The Viscount's Wife</u> (Book 4)

<u>The Window to the Heart Saga

Trilogy Box Set</u>

<u>The Window to the Heart Saga

Spin-off Books Box Set</u>

<u>The Window to the Heart Saga

Complete Collection Box Set</u>

The Lawkeepers is a multi-author series alternating between historical westerns and contemporary westerns featuring law enforcement heroes that span multiple agencies and generations. Join bestselling author Jenna Brandt and many others as they weave captivating, sweet and inspirational stories of romance and suspense between the lawkeepers — and the women who love them. The Lawkeepers is a world like no other; a world where lawkeepers and heroes are honored with unforgettable stories, characters, and love. Jenna's Lawkeeper books:

Historical

Lawfully Loved-Texas Sheriff

Lawfully Wanted-Bounty Hunter

Lawfully Forgiven-Texas Ranger

Lawfully Avenged-US Marshal

Lawfully Covert-Spies

Lawfully Historical Box Set

Contemporary

Lawfully Adored-K-9

Lawfully Wedded-K-9

Lawfully Treasured-SWAT

Lawfully Dashing-Female Cop/Christmas

Lawfully Devoted-Billionaire Bodyguard/K-9

Lawfully Heroic-Military Police

Lawfully Contemporary Box Set

Billionaire Birthday Club is an exclusive resort—for the billionaire who appears to have everything but secretly wants more. After filling out a confidential survey, a curated celebration is waiting on the island to make their birthday wishes come true!

<u>The Billionaire's Birthday Wish</u>

<u>The Billionaire's Birthday Surprise</u>

Billionaires of Manhattan Series

The billionaires that live in Manhattan and the women who love them. If you love epic dates, grand romantic gestures, and men in suits with hearts of gold, then these are books are perfect for you.

<u>Waiting on the Billionaire</u>

<u>Nanny for the Billionaire</u>

<u>Merging with the Billionaire</u>

<u>(Entire series available on audiobook)</u>

Second Chance Islands-What's better than billionaires on islands? How about billionaires finding second chances at life, love, and redemption while on one.

The Billionaire's Repeat

(Free the you join my newsletter)

Disaster City Search and Rescue

Step into the world of Disaster City Search and Rescue, where officers, firefighters, military, and medics, train and work alongside each other with the dogs they love, to do the most dangerous job of all — help lost and injured victims find their way home.

Holliday Islands Resort-After growing his Alaskan resort empire into the "honeymooner's paradise of the world," Gordon Holliday is ready to retire. But there's no way he can cruise the globe in his luxury yacht until his sons are groomed and polished into proper executives to take his place. There's just one catch: He's convinced their biggest current job requirement is marriage!

<u>Comet's Blazing Love</u>

For more information about Jenna Brandt, signup for her <u>Newsletter</u> or visit her on any of her social media platforms:

<u>www.JennaBrandt.com</u>

<u>www.facebook.com/JennaBrandtAuthor</u>

<u>Jenna Brandt's Reader Group</u>

<u>www.twitter.com/JennaDBrandt</u>

<u>www.instagram.com/jennabrandtauthor</u>

**Sign-up for my newsletter and get a FREE
book and a FREE short story.**

**Join my Reader's Group, Jenna's Joyful Page
Turners, and get access to exclusive content
and contests.**

**Join my multi-author reader's group,
Heroes and Hunks, for fun with some of
your favorite sweet authors**

ACKNOWLEDGMENTS

My writing journey would not be possible without those who supported me. Since I can remember, writing is the only thing I love to do, and my deepest desire is to share my talent with others.

First and foremost, I am eternally grateful to Jesus, my lord and savior, who created me with this "writing bug" DNA.

In addition, many thanks go to:

My husband, Dustin, and three daughters, Katie, Julie, and Nikki, for loving me and supporting me during all my late-night writing marathons and coffee-infused mornings.

My mother, Connie, for being my first and most honest critic, now and always. As a little girl, sleeping under your desk during late-night deadlines for the local paper showed me what being a dedicated writer looked like.

My angels in heaven: my grandmother, who passed away in 2001; my infant son, Dylan, who was taken by SIDS six years ago; and my father, who left us four years ago.

To Ginny Sterling and Jo Grafford, my best writing buddies, my comrades-in-arms, my sounding boards, my voices of reason, my partners in all things author. I love you ladies so much.

To my ARC Angels and Beta Bells for taking the time to read my story and give valuable feedback.

And lastly, but so important, to my dedicated readers, who have shared their love of my books with others, helping to spread the words about my stories. Your devotion means a great deal.

Jenna Brandt is an international bestselling and award-winning author who writes historical and contemporary romance. Her historical books span from Victorian to Western eras and all of her books have elements of romance, suspense and faith. She has her own best-selling historical series, Window to the Heart Saga and Civil War Brides, as well as contemporary series, Billionaires of Manhattan and Second Chance Islands. Additionally, she's created two best-selling multi-author series, The Lawkeepers and Disaster City Search and Rescue based off the life of her husband in law enforcement as well as Billionaire Birthday Club. Both of her books, Waiting on the Billionaire and Lawfully Treasured, were voted into the Top 50 Indie Books of 2018 on Readfreely.com.

She's been an avid reader since she could hold a book and started writing stories almost as early. She's been published in several newspapers as well as edited for multiple papers, and graduated with her Bachelor of Arts degree in English from Bethany College where she was the Editor-in-Chief of the newspaper. Her first blog was published on The Mighty website, Yahoo Parenting and The Grief Toolbox as well as featured on the ABC News, CNN Health, and Good Morning America websites. She's also a member of the American Christian Fiction Writers (ACFW) association.

Writing is her passion, but she also enjoys date nights with her hubby, cooking from scratch, watching movies on Netflix, reading books by her author friends, and engaging in social media with her readers. Her three young daughters keep her busy with Girl Scout activities, going to the mall, and playing at the park where they live in the Central Valley of California. She summers on the Golden Central Coast where she finds endless inspiration for her romance books. She's also active in her local church where she volunteers on their first impressions team.